VILLAIN OF THE PIECE

Geonn Cannon

Supposed Crimes LLC • Matthews, North Carolina

All Rights Reserved
Copyright © 2022 Geonn Cannon

Published in the United States.

ISBN: 978-1-952150-30-2

www.supposedcrimes.com

This book is typeset in Goudy Old Style.

VILLAIN OF THE PIECE

PROLOGUE

THE LIGHTS *stay on. Music plays, the same song. Over and over. David Bowie, Queen Bitch. She loves David Bowie. Sometimes it starts over in the middle, sometimes it skips. She wasn't prepared for how jarring that would be. Her mind rebels and she reacts physically when it happens. A twitch, a flinch. But she doesn't say anything.*

She is on her knees. Her arms are bound behind her back. She's slumped forward but she can't lay down because of the strip of leather around her neck. It's attached to a chain, which is attached to the ceiling, and if she leans too far forward, it chokes her. She could end things that way, but they're monitoring her. They'll stop her before it gets to that point. Bring her back.

They've already done it twice. People rushing to save her life so they can spend more time killing her. Restarting her heart. Bandaging her wounds. Over and over again.

The door opens.

The room beyond is a black void. Or maybe her eyes are just broken by the white walls, white floor, white clothes, white bed, bright white light.

The men who come in are dressed all in black. It's like they don't exist. Cut-outs in reality. There aren't always five, but there's always at least two. Today there are three.

"Hello," says the only one who talks. He never says good morning or good evening. He never gives her an idea of what time it might actually be. But she smells coffee on him, shampoo on one of the others. Morning. She

keeps this information for herself, like a gem.

Talking Man crouches in front of her. He grabs her hair and lifts her head roughly. She looks through his featureless black mask as he examines the damage from his last visit.

"Still healing," he says and drops her head. "So no face this time. Hands? Let's go with the hands."

Shampoo walks around behind her.

Talking Man stands up. "He doesn't have to do anything. He hates this almost as much as you do. I'm the only one who kind of enjoys it, but even I admit to being a little bored at this point. So I'll make you a deal. You don't have to give us everything. Just one thing. One contact. One file name. One bank account number. You just have to give us one, and nothing will happen. We'll leave, grateful, and you get to focus on healing for a little while longer. How does that sound?"

She spits on the floor. There's blood in it, and it joins the stained spot where she's spit a dozen or a hundred times before.

Talking Man sighs. "Break two of her fingers."

Shampoo bends down to take one of her hands in his. She anticipates the pain but doesn't brace for it. She can handle the pain. Eventually it will go away. She'll heal or she'll die, and she won't give them the satisfaction of screaming. She bites hard on her cheek to stop herself from it. She trembles from holding it in. Tears are in her eyes.

And then she has two broken fingers. They throb. But she can feel the frustration coming from the men as they circle around her.

"The offer stands. Just one name. Any of your contacts. Hell, there must have been someone who rubbed you the wrong way. Some asshole. Give us his name to save yourself some pain."

She stares and stays silent.

"You're going to give us everything eventually, Catriona. You'll do it gladly."

She sits up, creating slack in her collar. She keeps her spine straight and her shoulders square. Waiting, almost a willing participant in her own torture at this point. Talking Man makes a harsh gesture and turns away. She can almost smell his fury.

Queen Bitch starts over again. David Bowie wails. Shampoo breaks another one of her fingers.

Catriona Hendrix remains silent.

CHAPTER ONE

"FIFTEEN MORE days," Whitney Mercer muttered under her breath. "Just give me fifteen more days and then you'll get treated like it's your birthday. Okay?" She twisted the screwdriver and looked at the pressure gauge. The needle wavered toward 12 PSI and then held. Whitney closed her eyes, gave a relieved sigh, and patted the cylinder. "Good boy."

The pressure started slipping a few months ago, leading to irritated customers complaining about flat beer. Which led to debating whether giving them free drinks was a bigger discount than risking a bad review online. She hated online reviews. So easy for anyone to just leave lies. Or, occasionally, she had to admit, the truth.

For a while she'd been able to give the bolt a quick twist and the problem would be solved. But lately the pressure was slipping a lot more frequently, and she found herself forced to keep a screwdriver handy at all times just in case she had to crouch down and nudge it a little. She knew she needed a whole new regulator, and hopefully she would have enough mad money at the end of the month to swing one. If she didn't... well, one more month of mediocre drinks wouldn't killed anyone.

Whitney was preoccupied when she came out of the kitchen, thinking about what she could possibly cut from her budget, so it took her a few seconds to realize someone was standing in the doorway to the bar. The room was dark, and the light filtering through the smoky windows along the front of the building turned the woman into a hazy silhouette.

"Sorry," the woman said. "Are you open?"

"Technically," Whitney said, coming closer to the taps. "What can I get for you?"

The woman came closer. She was wearing a denim jacket and a turtleneck. Her red hair had escaped her knit cap and gathered in mounds on her shoulders. A leather messenger bag hung low on her hip, the strap cutting across her chest. She looked mid to late thirties, with the kind of pink complexion redheads tended to get when they spent too much time in the sun.

"Actually," she said, "I'm here about the sign in your window about the apartment for rent upstairs."

For a second, Whitney thought she was joking. The sign had been there for over three years, since the previous tenant died in his sleep.

"Seriously? You know this isn't the best part of town." She mentally yelled at herself for trying to ruin her chances. "And the apartment kind of sucks." She raged in her own mind. "There's a reason it's only a thousand per month. It's the cheapest place in a five mile radius and nobody's even biting. That should tell you something."

"Tells me exactly what I need to know, honestly." She sounded weirdly breathless, like she was working against a clock. "Does it have a kitchen? Bathroom? Bed?"

"Yeah..."

The woman approached the bar and reached into the satchel. "I can pay first month, last month... is there a security deposit?"

Whitney was trying to wrap her mind around the fact she was about to get handed two thousand dollars. "Uh, yeah, that's... that part is, um, five hundred."

The woman put three stacks of cash on the bar. "First and last month, security deposit." She added two more stacks. "And I'll double it if you don't let anyone know the apartment is taken."

Whitney pulled her eyes away from the cash. "What?"

"No name on the mailbox outside. And keep the sign up. If you have it listed anywhere, keep that up. If anyone calls asking about it~"

"That's not going to happen." Whitney felt like she was drunk.

"You're the first person who has even mentioned it in a year."

"Good. That's great. But as far as anyone else is concerned, that apartment is empty. Okay?"

Whitney bristled at the idea of looking this gift horse in the mouth, but she knew when things sounded too good to be true. "What's going on? Who are you? If this is something illegal..."

"Nothing illegal. And nothing... Well..." She looked toward the windows and shrugged. "Nothing more dangerous than what you're already used to dealing with in this neighborhood."

Five grand sat on the bar between them. Whitney's hands rested on the bar, fingers poised like spider legs, ready to reach out and grab the cash before the woman could come to her senses.

"Why would you want to live here if you have this kind of cash?"

She scratched the side of her nose. "Two things. First, cash doesn't always mean you have options. Sometimes the cheapest way is the smartest. Second, it's not for me. It's for my boss. She needs a place to..." Her mind wandered, searching for the right word. Or maybe for the right synonym that wouldn't raise alarm bells. "A place to recuperate."

"Drugs? Something illegal?"

"No, nothing like that. She was... hurt. She's recovering."

Everything about the situation stank. Whitney looked down at the cash. She thought about the regulator, about how often she had to get out the damn screwdriver and adjust the pressure. How long would it be before she couldn't get it right anymore and she just had to serve flat beer? The bar didn't have nearly enough going for it to justify that kind of reputation. Five grand would fix the whole problem in a snap.

"Okay," she said.

"Okay?" Surprise lit up the woman's face, her eyes widening with relief.

Whitney nodded. "I need the cash, and it's not like the place is making itself useful otherwise. If someone wants to pay me to hide out there... you're sure it's not illegal?"

"Nothing illegal." She hesitated. "Nothing the cops will care about."

Alarms went off again, but the decision was already made. Whitney could already feel the money in her pocket. She had no interest in backtracking now and losing it.

"You can get to the apartment from the door by the alley. It's unlocked, stairs lead up to the second floor. The apartment is semi-furnished. It's pretty bare bones."

"That's fine." The woman pushed the money across the bar. "Thank you. You have no idea how much you've helped."

Whitney looked at the money, distracted enough that the woman almost vanished as mysteriously as she'd appeared. She stopped her at the door with a sharp, "Hey!"

The woman turned. "Is something wrong?"

"I can promise I won't change the mailbox, but if someone's going to be living in my building, I need to know her name."

The woman looked at the ground, one hand on the door. "Hendrix," she said finally. "Catriona Hendrix."

And then she left. Whitney moved quickly, stepping out from behind the bar and hurrying to the front window. She rubbed away the cobwebs and grime from one corner and peeked out.

A car was parked at the curb. Whitney watched as the mystery woman opened the back door and crouched down. She struggled with something for a moment, then stood up hauling a human-shaped bundle of black clothes from the car. The other person stumbled, and the woman caught her. She put the shrouded woman's arm around her neck and they stood together. Whitney watched them make slow progress across the sidewalk to the exterior door. A few seconds later, she heard the heavy thud of footsteps on the stairs. One of the women, maybe both, had a hand against the wall for balance as they made glacial upward progress.

Whitney realized she still had the apartment key. "Shit."

She patted her pockets as she hurried across the bar. She raced up the interior stairs and arrived at the landing well before her new tenants. She was waiting by the apartment door when they finally reached the top. The woman who had arranged the rental tensed at the sight of her, placing one hand against the other woman's shoulder to stop her.

The black shroud was actually a hoodie underneath a duster. The hood was pulled up, and the woman was wearing a Seattle Kraken baseball cap which was pulled low enough to obscure her face. Still, Whitney could see a pair of large sunglasses and what looked like gauze wrapped around her jaw.

Whitney swallowed a lump of anxiety and held up her keyring. "Everything happened so fast, I didn't even give you the key."

"Oh." The woman relaxed slightly. "Right."

Whitney turned to unlock the door. "There's a spare. Uh, it's in my apartment. So this one will be yours. Hers. Uh, it... it can be..." She coughed and pushed the door open. "There you are."

The two women approached. The shrouded one (*Catriona?*) was dragging her right foot. The other woman guided her, half-carried her, inside.

As promised, the apartment wasn't much. A kitchen directly ahead of the entrance, a bare mattress on a steel frame behind the door, and a space that could be set up with a couch and a TV on the opposite side of the apartment. Whitney watched the women shuffle across the floor. Catriona gingerly lowered herself onto the bed, her entire body tense as if she thought it might collapse under her. Whitney wasn't confident enough in its reliability to assure her it wouldn't.

"There's a laundromat down the street. If, ah, you need me to take it there for you, I'd be happy to take her things when I take mine."

"That's very kind," said the woman who had done all the speaking. "I'll be around to help her with that sort of thing."

"Oh, will you be living here too?"

"No."

Whitney waited for more, but the woman focused on helping Catriona lie down. "Okay, then. My apartment is at the end of the hall. The red door. If you need anything or have any questions, let me know."

"Okay. Thank you for everything."

"Sure." She took a step back. "Oh, the key..."

She fumbled with the keyring. The woman straightened and moved toward her, holding out an arm to indicate they should go out into the hall. Whitney was grateful to escape the apartment. The woman pulled the door halfway shut behind her.

"Can I ask what happened to her?" Whitney asked softly.

"No."

Whitney raised an eyebrow.

"Is that a dealbreaker?"

Whitney thought about it. "No. Is she going to be okay?"

This time the other woman thought. She shrugged. "I don't know. I think so."

The key finally came loose, and Whitney held it out to her. "You can make a copy of that for yourself if you need it."

"Thank you." She took the key and started to go back into the apartment.

"My name is Whitney." The woman stopped. "This is my home. And my work. If you're going to be spending time here, I should at least know your name, don't you think?"

The woman made a face that Whitney interpreted as 'you have a point.' She relaxed slightly and stepped back into the hallway, holding out her hand.

"Maureen Rigby."

Whitney gripped her hand. "Whitney Mercer. I hope your friend is going to be okay."

Maureen sighed. "I don't know. It's going to be hard, and it could go either way. But it's a lot more likely now than it was this morning, thanks to you."

"I hope so. Uh, there's a map of the neighborhood somewhere downstairs. Restaurants, grocery stores, the necessities. And places she might want to avoid. Like I said, it's not the greatest neighborhood. I'll find it and slip a copy under the door."

"I appreciate it. Thank you again. For everything."

"Of course."

Maureen opened the apartment door just wide enough to get inside and shut it behind her. Whitney stared at the chipping paint and the faded area that had once been covered by a gold 3 that had vanished at least a decade ago. She drummed her hand against her thigh, trying to wrap her brain around her new mysterious tenant. Something terrible had obviously happened to her. Would it follow her? Was some horror about to come crashing through her life? She hoped whatever headaches Catriona Hendrix brought were worth a new regulator.

Whitney remembered that she'd left five grand sitting on the bar, the front door unlocked, and swore as she raced for the stairs. For once she hoped she hadn't gotten any customers.

***

The Whipjack Tavern was located in South Park, a forgotten and much-maligned neighborhood clinging to the very bottom edge of West Seattle. The soil, the air, and even the Duwamish River that made up their northeastern border were full of poison from the industrial works that had helped turn the city into one of the wealthiest in the US.

If Downtown was the Emerald City, then South Park was the Wicked Witch's castle.

Fortunately being in a less-desirable part of town was great for a bar's business. Whipjack was open from three in the afternoon until two in the morning. It was never crowded, but Whitney could count on a handful of regulars showing up at their usual times. The day her new tenant arrived, there were enough patrons to keep her mind from wandering to just what she'd gotten involved in. When things did get slow, she used her phone to search local news for stories involving a woman who had gone missing. She found some car accidents and a break-in, but none of it seemed to fit. She started to search for the woman's name, but stopped with her thumb over the keyboard on the screen. What if there were people looking for Catriona Hendrix, and they were monitoring searches? What if as soon as she hit "Go," some computer somewhere went "ping" and a shady government agent said, "Gotcha."

"That's just in the movies, right?"

The old man at the end of the bar looked up. "What's in the movies?"

Whitney shook her head and slipped her phone into her pocket. "Nothing. I'm just being paranoid. Can I get you a refill?"

He pushed his glass toward her. "As long as it's not flat."

"It's not flat," she said. "And I'm getting it fixed."

"Uh huh."

She decided against doing the search. She probably was just being paranoid, but she didn't plan on searching for such a unique name until she felt more comfortable about it.

Her second bartender, Violet, came in at nine. Violet was a student at UW and seemed to be constantly running between classes, the library, and one of her two jobs. She exhaled an apology to Whitney as she swept behind the bar and went into the kitchen to drop her bags off in the little kitchen. Whitney followed and caught up with her next to the stove.

Violet was putting on an apron and looked up sheepishly as she tied the strings behind her. "I know. Ten minutes late. Again. I swear I kept my eye on the clock, but the traffic—"

Whitney stopped her with a wave of her hand. "I don't care." She pulled some folded bills out of her pocket. She held it up so Violet could see, then placed it in her hand. "I want you to take this."

"How much—"

"Five hundred."

Violet's eyes widened. "Why?"

"For all the times I've been a week late with your paycheck and you didn't quit. Because if the customers didn't tip well, you wouldn't even be making minimum wage. I've owed you a raise for months now, but you've stuck with me. I want you to know how much I appreciate it. And this isn't a bribe, okay? If you find a better paying job, I don't want this to guilt you into staying."

Violet looked like she was on the verge of tears. "I don't want to leave. I-I-I study when things are slow, and I don't know any other boss who would just brush off how many times per week I show up late. I can't take this money." She held it out. "I know how tight things are."

"Things are a lot looser right now. I can't talk about it. But I think five hundred is a nice balance between what I can afford and what you actually deserve. The bills are paid. I called someone to come take a look at that piece of shit regulator. I want to make sure you're taken care of, too. Take the money. Please."

Violet pressed her lips together and looked down at the money, then stuck it in her pocket. "Thank you, Whitney."

"I appreciate you. You've been a real lifesaver. Now get out there and start your shift. I'm not paying you to stand here and get all sentimental."

Violet laughed and stepped forward, quickly pressing her shoulder against Whitney's in a not-quite hug. "Thank you. This money is going to be really helpful."

"I'm sure."

Violet stopped at the kitchen door. "Are you going to tell me where it came from?"

Whitney shook her head. "I'm not sure I'm allowed."

"Hm. Mysterious." She knocked on the wall next to the door and went out to start her shift.

Whitney took a breath and blew it out, her hands on her hips. She looked up at the ceiling and tried to listen for sounds of someone moving around above her. It had been eerily silent all day. Given how Hendrix had been moving earlier, she probably wouldn't be getting out of bed for anything short of an emergency. She decided she would take the same strategy. Unless a reason presented itself, she wasn't going to waste time thinking about her new tenant.

With Violet tending bar, Whitney opened the kitchen and started taking food orders. An hour later she was at the stove cooking an egg sandwich for one of their regulars when Violet called her out to the front. Whitney suddenly remembered what day it was and knew exactly what was wrong. She resisted the urge to swear, finished the sandwich, and took it out to the customer without looking toward the front booth.

By the time she got behind the bar, Peter Bridgeman had gotten up and was waiting like he was any other customer. He smiled brightly at her. She glared at him and punched her code into the cash register and opened the cash drawer.

"Not even a hello?"

"Is this a social call?" she asked as she took out the envelope she kept tucked under the rest of the money. A thousand dollars, collected in dribs and drabs over the past month. It hurt a little less than usual this time, what with her current windfall, but she still hated the fact she had to hand it over.

Bridgeman took the envelope and opened the flap to count it. "Couldn't throw in a couple Franklins? Damn. Some of these look like you pulled them out of the trash."

"You want crisp bills, go to the bank."

He raised an eyebrow and looked at her without raising his head. "You know how much it costs to replace a broken window? Or you could have guys in here every night with guns demanding everything else in the register."

"Yeah. You're a saint. You're selling elephant repellent, and hey! Look, there's no elephants, so you must be doing a good job."

Bridgeman shrugged and pocketed the cash. "Why don't you ask that little barber shop on the corner if there are any elephants. They got robbed three times last month. Every mirror in the place shattered. At least that's what I heard. We could've stopped it from happening. The owner is paying again, so the next time someone thinks about going after that place, my friends will step in. We're providing a valuable community service."

"And you would have just happened to be in the right place at the right time to stop them if he had been paying you."

"We're like Batman that way." He had the audacity to wink at her.

Whitney had to resist the urge to slug him in the face. "You should probably leave if you're not going to order anything."

Bridgeman chuckled and pushed away from the bar. He waved over his shoulder as he headed for the door. "See you next month, Whitney."

When he was gone, Violet said, "If you need a little of that money back—"

"No," Whitney said immediately. "I factored this into my budget. That money is yours."

"I hate that guy. He's so... smug. Someone should do something about *him*."

Whitney sighed. "Yeah. Who is going to protect us from the protectors?"

CHAPTER TWO

FOR THE next few weeks, it was easy for Whitney to forget she had a tenant. Catriona Hendrix, whatever else she might have been, was essentially a ghost. She heard movement from time to time. Footsteps going to the bathroom, coughing, the scrape of chair legs on hardwood. Whitney worked until five in the morning, so she was usually trying sleep when Maureen came for her early-morning visits. Even then, she only ever heard the one voice.

"Maybe it's a *Psycho*. You know, like the movie? Doesn't the creepy guy in that have his mother's skeleton in the attic or something? And he dresses up like her and fakes her voice?"

"But I saw her when she first moved in. Sort of. And we've both heard someone moving around even when Maureen isn't here," Whitney argued. "There's definitely someone up there."

They'd both looked up toward the ceiling as if they expected to hear a thump in response. As usual, nothing happened.

Eventually Whitney decided a quiet tenant was better than the alternative. Live and let live. She wasn't going to be a nosy landlady.

Another thing that made it easy to ignore her new neighbor was how quickly the money had vanished. Between fixing the regulator, paying Violet, and tending to a few other necessary repairs around the bar, she was already back to finessing the bills in order to make sure nothing slipped through the cracks. She'd planned to set aside some of the cash for Bridgeman so she wouldn't have to skim off the top of her profits, but that hadn't happened.

Exactly one month after she first came into the Whipjack Tavern, Maureen returned. This time she had a denim backpack slung over one shoulder, which she let drop down her arm so she could catch the strap. Whitney had been in the back but came out when she heard the door.

"You're back."

"I'm back," Maureen said, placing the bag on the bar. "In books and movies, they make it seem like rent is a monthly thing."

"That's usually how it works," Whitney confirmed.

She watched as Maureen took out a stack of bills and placed it next to the bag. Then she took out another stack and went for a third.

"Seriously?" Whitney said.

Maureen paused and looked at her, the picture of innocence. "Pardon?"

"Are you planning to give me another five grand?"

"That's what we agreed on last month."

"For first, last, security deposit." Whitney waved the money away, even though one side of her brain was already spending it. "The rent for this month is just a grand."

Maureen rested her hands on top of the bag. "We also agreed on keeping quiet. Keeping the apartment on the market. That deal is still good, right?"

"Of course. Even though I don't really understand it."

Maureen started stacking money again. "Let's call this a bonus, then, for keeping your word. Next month I'll go to the normal amount."

Whitney stepped forward. She was irrationally angry at this woman for throwing much-needed cash at her.

"What the hell is this? You just have this kind of money to throw around? You pay five times what the apartment is worth when you could be paying a fraction of that for an apartment in a building with actual security measures. Doorman. Cameras."

Maureen sighed. "That would be great. But it's not an option for reasons I don't~ I *can't* go into. She just needs a place to lie low for a while. The most important thing about this apartment is anonymity. It's just a room. No one to see me coming and going. No other neighbors poking their noses in. No building managers who ask a lot of questions. Those buildings have better security, but they also have paperwork. They have rules about who can rent their apartments and how they get paid. You think I could get a place in downtown Seattle with cash?"

"Probably not."

"Definitely not." She sighed and closed her eyes. "Please take the money. It's what she believes the apartment is worth. She wouldn't be paying you extra out of generosity or the kindness of her heart." She almost choke-laughed on the last part. "To her, this is strictly fair compensation."

Five thousand dollars. Whitney's fingers twitched. "Am I going to regret taking it?"

Maureen opened her mouth. Closed it. Pressed her lips together. "I can't definitively say no. But I can confidently say I don't think so. As long as you follow my requests."

"No name on the mailbox. The apartment is still available."

"Right."

Whitney surrendered. "Okay. Fine. But next month is the standard rent."

"I honestly can't promise that, either. I just give you what she gives me." Maureen's voice had just been tired, but now there was an edge of irritation. "Are you really fighting me on this? I can't believe I'm forcing five thousand dollars on you."

"It's not the money. It's the hope. Anticipation. I don't want to get to the point where I'm counting on five grand, then suddenly you don't show up. Suddenly the well goes dry. I don't want to rely on getting this every month."

Maureen softened. "I get that. That makes sense."

Whitney took the money and awkwardly tucked it into the front pocket of her apron. "I don't suppose you're willing to tell me anything else about her."

"Nothing to tell."

"There has to be something. The woman hasn't left the apartment since you brought her here. I barely hear any signs of life. Is she sick?"

Maureen said, "I really can't go into it. She's not sick. You don't have to worry about catching anything. She's just very antisocial at the best of times, and this is nowhere near the best of times for her."

"I know you stop by pretty much every day. I assume you bring her food? Groceries?"

"Yeah, I take care of what she needs."

Whitney nodded. "Is there anything I can do?"

Maureen shrugged and slung the bag's strap back over her shoulder. "Just what you're already doing. Best to treat her like a benevolent ghost that lives down the hall from you."

"So your advice is just try to ignore her."

"It's a good strategy. And trust me, you'll be much better off if you do."

Maureen touched a finger to her eyebrow and pulled the door open, sweeping out into the sunlight and letting the door swing shut behind her.

Whitney looked up toward the ceiling. "Ignore her. Well, it's worked so far..."

Still, even with the minimal impact the woman had on her life, Whitney was worried it wouldn't be long before ignoring her would be easier said than done.

****

The end of the month arrived a few days later. Whitney had Bridgeman's money set aside, ready and waiting for him to show up. It was a slow night, but still relatively early. It was only a little after ten o'clock but there were still no customers in sight. Violet was in the kitchen, and Whitney was behind the bar reading a book. Occasionally she looked toward the door as if trying to summon Bridgeman, to get it over with, or a customer, to give herself something to do. It was quieter than usual, as it had been all week, and she was grateful she had Maureen's bribery to help make the pay-off.

She thought the first thump was just her hearing things. The second thump could've been Violet cleaning something in the kitchen. The third was when Whitney looked up from her book and realized the sound was coming from the stairwell that led upstairs.

Someone was coming down.

Violet poked her head out of the kitchen. "Do you hear that?"

"Yeah. Stay in the kitchen."

"Do you think she's dangerous?"

Whitney started to say no, but she realized she didn't know if that would be a lie. "Just to be on the safe side."

The thumps continued making slow, rhythmic progress down. Whitney had tended bar for years but panicked and reverted to tropes she'd seen on television. She grabbed a rag and pretended to be wiping down the bar's surface when the thumping finally reached the bottom of the stairwell. The door opened slowly and Whitney finally got her first good look at her tenant.

Catriona Hendrix, if that was her real name, wore a black hoodie zipped all the way up to her throat. She wore a baseball cap under the hood, and a pair of sunglasses even though it was the middle of the night.

She moved cautiously, making sure each step landed solidly before she took the next. She kept one hand extended as if she expected to fall at any second. When she finally reached the farthest booth, she half-threw herself into the seat so she could face the door. She slumped back against the wall with the exhausted relief of someone who had just run a marathon and let out a sigh of relief.

Whitney hesitantly approached with the laminated one-sheet that served as her menu. Catriona didn't acknowledge her arrival next to the table. For a moment she was afraid the woman had died immediately after sitting down, but her chest rose and fell from the exertion of her descent.

"Hi. We haven't been properly introduced. I'm Whitney. I'm... well, I guess I'm your landlady."

The head lolled toward her. Whitney put the menu down in front of her.

"You can take your time with~"

Catriona pressed one finger down on a picture of a sausage egg and cheese biscuit. Then she moved it to the list of beverages and poked the last option.

"A breakfast biscuit and a milk?"

A slight lean forward seemed to be the closest thing to a nod she would get. Catriona leaned to one side, reached into her pocket, and pulled out a wad of wrinkled and torn bills. It was a far cry from the ATM-crisp money Maureen had been giving her. Catriona's hands trembled as she tried to straighten the money out, giving Whitney a chance to examine them closely.

Her fingers had been broken. All of them. The knuckles bulged, and the smallest finger on her right hand bent at an unnatural angle. The tips of two fingers on her left hand were wrapped in bandages smeared with dried blood. The sleeve of her hoodie had been pushed up high enough that Whitney could see what looked like rope burns.

"On the house," she said without expecting to.

Catriona's head tilted toward her. The question was implied in the set of her lips.

"Consider it a, uh, welcome to the building gift. Besides, your... your associate has been very generous and punctual with your rent. So as long as that continues, you can eat here for free. I'm pretty sure I'm still coming out on top."

Another forward lean, almost a bow.

"I'll get right on that for you. Keep the menu. Might as well get to know what we have to offer."

She went into the kitchen and discovered Violet had been eavesdropping. "Well?"

Whitney shook her head. "No idea. Maybe she doesn't speak English."

"She seemed to understand what you were saying well enough."

"I can understand Chinese and French because that's what my parents spoke, but I can't hold a conversation in it. If I went to Beijing, I would probably point at the menu."

Violet said, "Fair." She peeked around the pass-through. "She kind of scares me. Dressed all in black like that? Not talking?"

"Her fingers have all been broken, too."

"What?"

Whitney shrugged and started cooking. "No idea what that means, but she's been through it. Can you get her milk?"

Violet went to the fridge and poured a glass. She was about to take it out when they heard the bell over the door chime. Violet froze and looked back at Whitney, eyes wide with fear.

"Hello-o-o, Miss Mercer," Bridgeman called out.

"Take over here. I'll take the milk out."

"Be careful," Violet whispered.

Whitney nodded and took the glass out to the main room. Bridgeman was waiting near the cash register. Three younger men were standing by the door, slouching with their hands buried in their pockets, watching her as she crossed the room. She placed it on Whitney's table, ignoring Bridgeman until she was back behind the bar.

"An actual customer!" He rested his elbows on the bar and leaned forward. "This is the second time I've seen people actually in here. Wonders never cease."

She got out the envelope and dropped it down in front of him. "Will there be anything else?"

His shoulders slumped. He gave an exaggerated pout. "You never want to talk. Shoot the breeze."

"Order a drink," she said.

He grinned and handed the money to one of his goons. The envelope disappeared into the second man's denim jacket. Bridgeman straightened and rapped his knuckles on the bar.

"Maybe we should change it to five hundred every two weeks. It would give us a chance to see each other twice a month. We could really get to know each other."

Whitney narrowed her eyes at him in a non-smile. "Once is about all I can stomach, thanks."

Bridgeman clicked his tongue. "So rude..." He winked at her and made a motion with his head. His trio of friends took it to mean they were leaving. One opened the door and led the way outside. Whitney stared at the backs of their heads until they were gone.

Violet came out of the kitchen with Catriona's biscuit on a plate. "Why do those assholes always have to come by in the middle of the night?"

"That's when all the vermin come out."

She was about to tell Violet to deliver the biscuit before it got cold, but she was surprised by Catriona rising suddenly from the booth. She moved quickly, as if she hadn't just dragged herself down the stairs like it was a herculean effort. There was no hesitation in her stride, no hint that she was pained as she crossed to the door. She either didn't notice Whitney gawking at her or didn't care, because she didn't slow down before she shoved through the door and into the night.

"Hey, what..."

"Where~" Violet provided.

Catriona was out the door before either of them could manage to finish their questions. Whitney looked at Violet. Violet looked back at her, then down at the plate in her hand.

"What am I supposed to do with this?"

***

"I think she's got a crush on you."

Bridgeman laughed and thrust his elbow toward Colin. "You think? Maybe one of these days I'll slum it." His friends laughed, and he put up his hood. They were approaching the South Park Bridge, and he knew the wind off the Duwamish was going to be frigid. "It ain't gonna be any time soon, though. I got plenty of sweeties without wasting my time with some poor old lady."

"She ain't that old," David said.

"Old enough," Bridgeman said.

Their route was a long, exhausting walk, but they didn't have to be anywhere at a specific time. The place seemed to lock down tight around nine-thirty, and they had the streets mostly to themselves. No cars passed, and they were the only people on the street, but Bridgeman knew there were criminals and thieves lurking in the shadows. That's why he would never leave his car unattended in South Park even for the few minutes it took to run in and do their rounds. Walking suited him fine. Besides, his boys could use the exercise.

The neighborhood wasn't too bad in daylight. A little shabby and rundown, just like a hundred other small enclaves around Seattle. But once it got dark, you rarely went a half hour without hearing sirens. He could hear some now, in fact, and adjusted his pace to look less suspicious.

They reached the end of the road and passed the massive gears from the old bridge. They'd been repurposed as artistic flourishes when the city revamped the bridge a few years earlier, and Bridgeman always thought they made the place look way nicer than it actually was. This dump didn't deserve such a fancy-looking entry point. False advertising, that was all it was.

"Yo, B."

He glanced back to see Josh had slowed down, looking back the way they'd come. "What's up?"

"I think someone's following us, man."

"Probably just someone walking the same way. Don't get paranoid."

Josh looked back at them. "You guys go on. I'll just make sure no one's being stupid."

Bridgeman saluted. "You're a good man, Josh. C'mon, guys."

Josh moved to use the shadow of the gears as cover. Bridgeman and the others continued on. David glanced back, probably hoping to see Josh rough someone up.

"How many other places we gotta hit tonight?" David asked.

"Two more bars and the motel. We'll hit the strip club last. Give 'em a chance to earn back some of their money."

David and Colin laughed.

They stopped at the far end. There were security lights all along the length of the bridge, and they gathered under the glow of one to wait for Josh. David stuck his hands in his pockets. Colin paced in a tight circle. Bridgeman leaned against the pole, hands in his pockets, and looked back the way they'd come. No movement, no sound of footsteps, not even the sounds of Josh telling whoever had been following them to take another route.

"The fuck is taking him so long?" David muttered.

"Maybe it was a chick," Colin said. "Probably back there getting~"

He was interrupted by a splash from the river.

Bridgeman pushed away from the pole and craned his neck. The bridge curved just enough that he couldn't see the other side from where they were standing. Had he heard a yelp just before the splash? He hadn't really been paying attention but in retrospect it seemed likely. Or maybe his mind was playing tricks on him.

"What the hell just happened?"

"Something went in the water, sounded like," Colin said, tensing for a fight.

David said, "Should we go take a look?"

Bridgeman pressed his lips together and worked his jaw as he considered the question. He started back the way they'd come, motioned for Colin and David to fall in behind him. They marched onto the bridge, going just as far as they had to in order to see the other side of the Duwamish. When they could see the large gears, Bridgeman stopped. Colin and David bumped into him on either side, but none of them seemed to notice the collision.

Someone dressed all in black stood under one of the security lights. No threatening pose. No weapons that Bridgeman could see. Just a person. Standing there. A cutout of black against the rest of the night. They were just standing there.

"Who the hell is that?" Colin asked softly. "Where's Josh?"

Bridgeman furrowed his brow and sniffed, flicking his thumb against his nose. He started walking again.

"Let's go ask him."

Walking hurt like hell. Anger helped her push through the pain.

Catriona had been going crazy in the apartment. She wanted food that hadn't been microwaved, even if she wasn't certain she would be able to chew it properly. Getting downstairs had felt like an Olympic trial. She had seen the pity on that woman's face, and she hated it. But she appreciated the free food. And then these punks had come sauntering in like they owned the place. They took an envelope of cash like it was their inheritance.

A protection scam. In this day and age, these stupid motherfuckers were running one of the laziest cons in the book. She wondered how much they earned in a given month.

She'd been halfway out the door before she realized she was moving. It only clicked then because she became aware of the pain in her feet, her knees, her lower back. But she kept going. Some primal instinct had set her off, and she couldn't back down now. She forced herself to stand up straight and tall. She had to hope they weren't going far.

She reached the bridge and saw one of the guys coming back toward her. It was the one with the buzzcut. She didn't change her pace, knowing she would stumble if she tried. She lined herself up on the walkway so the guy would either have to move out of her way or collide with her.

"I think you should find another way home tonight, okay?" Buzzcut said when she was close enough that he didn't have to raise his voice. The threat was clear enough, however, and he stopped walking like a stanchion in front of her.

Catriona didn't stop or slow down.

"Hey, did you hear me?"

She was close enough now that he could grab her. He brought his hands up to grab her arms. She turned sideways, dropped her shoulder, and slammed into his sternum like a linebacker. He fell back and she swung her elbow up into his stomach. She'd already knocked the wind out of him, so he only managed a meager 'irk' when she chopped his throat with the side of her hand. He bent double and she slipped her arm around his neck, patted down his pockets for the money she'd seen the bar owner hand over. He didn't have it.

"Dead... bitch," he wheezed.

She'd faced tougher odd, but given her current condition, there was a good chance he wasn't wrong. She dragged him to the railing and peered over. Water. Maybe it would kill him, maybe he'd survive. Whatever happened, he'd be out of the way. She dropped her other hand down and grabbed him roughly by the crotch, bent at the knees, and hoisted him up.

He realized what she was doing when he was halfway over the rail. He grabbed at her, trying to pull her with him, but he was already over. She let go of his crotch and punched him in the side of the head. His hand flexed, he let go of her, and suddenly his weight dropped away from her. His fall was eerily silent, punctuated by a surprisingly small splash.

Catriona pushed away from the railing and looked toward the other side of the bridge. They would've heard that. They would come looking for their fallen friend.

She positioned herself under the security light and did a quick inventory of her injuries. She ached everywhere. She was afraid a few of her stitches might have opened. She felt blood inside her clothes. Not much, but enough. Reena would be pissed. She forced herself to stand as upright as possible. Arms at her sides. Hands relaxed, but with the fingers curled. She rubbed her thumbs across the pads of her fingers.

Her legs were steel beams. Her spine was a rod impaled in the concrete. Deep breaths. Steady.

The other goons came around the curve of the bridge. They stopped and stared at her.

Catriona stared back.

She watched them puff themselves up. Cats going fluffy and raising their tails to look bigger to a predator. Finally the leader started walking again. Many things were immediately apparent to her during their approach.

They were unarmed.

They didn't expect to actually fight. Every step was taken with the intent of intimidation, trying to scare off an opponent.

Two of them were just drones. They would do whatever their leader told them to do, and taking him out would render them useless. Their threat level was entirely dependent on the front man.

The front man had never been in a fight before. Not a real one.

He looked past her. He looked to either side, and he cupped his right fist in his left hand, popping the knuckles, and locked eyes on her.

"What did you do with my boy?"

She stared at him. She was still wearing her sunglasses, baseball cap, hoodie.

He leaned closer. Narrowed his eyes. "Yo, is this just a mannequin or some shit?" He brought his hand up to snap his fingers in front of her face.

Three seconds later, he was on his knees in front of her, his hand twisted backward in Catriona's grip. The backup goons backed up in shock, neither of them exactly sure what had just happened. Catriona held the front man's arm at the accurately-named breaking point just long enough for the pain to break through his shock so he would realize the position he was in. He opened his mouth to scream. That was when she pushed it and broke his wrist.

She put her foot on his chest and kicked him back. Goon One tried to grab him. Goon Two went for Catriona. He tripped over his leader's foot and went sprawling. Catriona only had to step out of his way and watch at his skull bounced off the pavement. She crouched down and patted his pockets. She found the envelope of money in his jacket, along with several others. She took one and slipped it into her own pockets.

"Bitch!"

He might have gotten the drop on her if he hadn't announced his attack. But since she knew he was coming, she twisted at the waist and shot her fist straight out toward where she assumed his face would be. Her knuckles met his nose. Bones crunches, and she wasn't sure if they were his or hers. Pain shot up her arm but she stayed upright while he went down with a spray of blood.

She took a step back so she could see all three of the fallen men. None seemed capable of a second attack, but she needed to be certain before walking away.

"You're dead." The front man's threat was tempered by the fact he sounded like he was moments away from tears, hunched over and cradling his hand.

Catriona walked to him and bent down so she could look into his eyes. He flinched, and she knew he saw it happen in the reflection from her sunglasses.

She held up one finger. He flinched again, and she knew he'd gotten the message: one blow, one hit, was all it took for her to completely take him out of the fight.

She straightened and turned her back on him.

She didn't bother looking back to see if they were following her.

CHAPTER THREE

THE ENVELOPE of money hit the bar with a heavy thud. Whitney stared at it, then looked at the woman in black who had dropped it and kept walking. Violet had left the biscuit on the counter, and Catriona picked it up as she passed, continuing on to the booth she'd vacated.

She was moving easier now, but it was obvious that she was still in tremendous pain. Sitting down looked like it was a tremendous relief to her. Whitney tore her gaze away from the returning stranger and looked at the money again.

"What is this?" she asked.

No response.

"What did you do? Are they going to come back here and break my windows?" She looked toward the door, half expecting to see Bridgeman storm in. She came out from behind the bar and stood next to the table. "Do you think I didn't know it was a con? I'm not an idiot. That's why I pay. Because this money prevents me from stressing about what they might do. They could run this place out of business if they wanted. They could send goons here tomorrow to harass my customers. They could have me robbed every night for a week. Giving them the money keeps them satisfied. It means I only have to worry about them one night every month and go on with my life the rest of the time."

Catriona had carefully broken apart her biscuit. Her fingers were stiff and seemed darker as she brought one piece of biscuit to her mouth and pressed it between her lips. She chewed carefully. The sunglasses were aimed at the empty seat across from her, as if Whitney wasn't even there.

"I... I know you were just trying to help. I do appreciate that. But whatever you did may have just made things a hundred times worse. I hope you understand that."

Catriona finally lifted her head. Whitney felt like the other woman was finally acknowledging her, even though the glasses didn't give anything away.

Whitney finally gave up waiting for any kind of response and walked away. She retrieved the envelope and checked inside. A thousand dollars in various denominations, all of it looking as beaten-up and wrinkled as the cash she'd given Bridgeman. She couldn't guarantee it was the same envelope she had just handed over, but she was pretty sure everyone paid the same fee, so it didn't matter if it was the exact same cash.

So the question became *how?* The woman could barely walk down the stairs. She couldn't eat a biscuit properly. She was eating with her right hand, while the left lay on the table like it was made of rubber. She only knew it was real because the fingers were trembling. Whitney didn't believe she could make it back upstairs unassisted, let alone intimidate Bridgeman and his crew.

Whatever had happened, she clearly wasn't going to get an answer from Catriona. She would probably hear about it soon enough when Bridgeman decided how he was going to punish her. A motel had once refused to pay, and the windows of every car in their parking lot paid the price. A night clerk had witnessed the vandalism and went to stop it. He was rewarded with a beating that put him in the hospital.

Bridgeman wasn't the most creative guy in the world, but his response didn't have to be clever to cause mayhem in her life. She tucked the money back in the crevice between the cash register and the wall, hoping and praying the Bridgeman gave her a chance to make amends before he unleashed whatever hell he came up with. Maybe she'd have to pay double, but she had enough from Maureen that it wouldn't be too much of a blow to her bank account.

She looked back at the booth where Catriona was still pecking at her food like a human-sized crow. She was starting to wonder if Maureen was really paying an exorbitant amount for rent, or if her new tenant was really enough trouble to make the price tag a bargain.

***

It took Catriona nearly an hour to finish her meal. She remained in the booth for another few minutes before she pushed herself up and shuffled back to the stairs. She was again moving like an elderly woman, as if every step was agony. A few customers had drifted in during the time she was there, but none of them paid much attention to the silent woman and her breakfast. Whitney had kept an eye on her as much as possible, enough that she was convinced there was nothing to see. The woman would break off a piece of bread, bring it to her mouth, press it between her lips or open her mouth just enough to pop it on her tongue, and then she would spend a good minute chewing. It almost looked meditative, but it was clear that she was trying to avoid pain.

Whitney closed a little after two in the morning, escorting her last customer out and locking the door behind him. She spent a little time cleaning before she headed upstairs. The night was busy enough that her encounter with Catriona had been pushed to the back of her mind. It came rushing back when she got to the top of the stairs and saw the other apartment door.

She thought about going over, knocking, trying to get a little more information about what had happened. She decided against it. Even if Catriona opened the door, Whitney doubted she would say anything no matter how the questions were framed. She shook her head and went into her own apartment. Better to just leave it.

The worst part about owning a bar was that it meant she was wide awake when the rest of the world was asleep. She changed out of her work clothes and put on the Orange Shirt. The shirt didn't fit her, forcing her to roll up her sleeves. And she admitted it was more than a little ratty now, and she'd been forced to mend both elbows and the seams at both shoulders, and there was a rectangular patch in the small of her back where she'd ripped it, but she would never throw it out. It was the Orange Shirt, her favorite, her most comfortable, and she wouldn't part with it any more than she would shave her eyebrows off.

Once she had some music playing - KZOK, "Seattle's ONLY classic rock station!" - she lit a joint and prepared to play detective. It was time to trying Googling her mysterious new neighbor.

She moved her laptop to the couch. It had been weeks and so far no one had come sniffing around, so maybe it was safe now.

Still, she took the most basic of security measures and opened an incognito window. An ex had once told her that was just a placebo. "The government pays *extra close* attention to that. They don't care what's in your official Google history. They only want to know what you're trying to hide." Whitney never bought that argument, but she was past the point of caring.

First she tried searching Catriona + Maureen. The names were unusual enough that she thought maybe she could narrow things down that way. No such luck.

With her fingers poised over the keyboard, she took a deep breath and finally typed in both names: Catriona Hendrix.

The top results were clarifying to make sure she hadn't misspelled one or both of the names. It occurred to her that Catriona *might* start with a K, and maybe Hendrix ended with 'cks,' but she didn't think so. She had nothing to base that on other than how Maureen had said the name, and she would have felt dumb justifying it to anyone. But she was fairly sure she'd gotten it correct.

Not that it mattered. She scrolled through the results, then double-checked the wrong ones, and no combination of any spelling returned anything that looked even close to right.

She slumped back against the couch and stared at the screen. She listened to the radio and tried to think of her next step. She also tried not to think about how, when, or why the Red Hot Chili Peppers qualified for a 'classic' rock station. *Californication* wasn't that old. It had come out in '99, and that was only... She winced. It was still ridiculous to have "Around the World" playing right after Joan Jett.

Maybe there was something in, or on, Maureen's car that could provide another lead. She would have to try and get a look at it the next time she came by.

She closed her eyes at some point, aware of the computer's weight on her lap but lacking the will or energy to move it. She felt herself drifting but told herself she was only resting for a minute, but then it felt more like five, and then she lost track. She hated sleeping sitting up. She told herself to get comfortable but her body, having been upright since noon, rebelled and stayed in its slack position. Her dozing eventually turned into full sleep despite the light being on. Her hands slipped off the keyboard, her head lolling against one shoulder.

And then there was a raised voice, and something hard slammed down on the floor.

Whitney jumped but managed to grab the computer before she bucked it off her lap. Her brain had been aware of something happened before it was startled back to consciousness, and now it raced to fill in the blanks. She'd heard a door, right? And the shout that woke her up hadn't been the first time the voice was raised. The fight had been going on for at least a few minutes.

She moved the computer to the coffee table and tiptoed across the living room to the shared wall. The voice belonged to Maureen; she was positive of that. It was also extremely clear that she was *pissed*. Whitney couldn't make out what she was saying, but it was easy to guess what had made her so mad.

The car, Whitney thought. This was her chance to look for more information. Even just glancing at the license plate might give her enough info to narrow things down.

She started moving before she could second guess herself. She was still just in her socks, but she didn't dare slow down to put on shoes. She opened the door as quietly as possible, peeked out into the hall, and then made the quietest dash she could to the top of the stairs. She caught a snippet of Maureen's diatribe as she passed Catriona's apartment.

"~completely reckless. You could have undone any progress you've managed to achieve~"

Whitney carefully, quietly, opened the door to the street and propped it open with a brick. She was very aware she was in her relaxing clothes when the first cold wind blew past her, but it was too late to back out now. She saw Maureen's car at the curb and went over to it, already scanning for anything that looked liked it might be a clue.

The Washington state license plate wasn't helpful at all, and she couldn't see anything that might narrow its origins down farther than that. It looked like an old junker, definitely not the sort of thing she'd expect for someone who had paid her ten grand in the space of a few weeks. Maybe it was part of their cover. No one would look twice at this thing unless they were parking enforcement.

It was the backseat that really caught her attention. There was a pile of blankets stretched across from one side to the other, and a stack of pillows against the driver's side door. The space between the front and back seats had been filled with clothes. Whitney got closer and saw toothpaste, a toothbrush, deodorant, and other hygienic products on the dashboard and scattered across the passenger seat.

She backed away from the car and went back to the door. Her mind raced with the implication of the car's contents as she went up. She thought about Maureen saying how few places would accept cash for rent, and even the hotels required credit cards and a paper trail. She was so distracted that she was unprepared when she reached the landing to find Maureen coming out of Catriona's apartment.

Both women froze and stared at each other. Maureen's face was red, and she quickly looked away, wiping at her eyes with the back of her hand. She was dressed in her usual uniform of warm clothes despite the fact it was the middle of the night.

"I was just taking out some trash," Whitney said, not that she needed an excuse to be doing anything in her own building.

Maureen nodded. "I was... Catriona texted me." The attempt to keep her voice steady only highlighted the stress she was under. "She needed some, uh, pain meds. Apparently she had a pretty eventful night."

Whitney moved closer, cautious. "Yeah, did she explain any of that to you? Because I saw part of it, and~"

"You saw it?" Maureen's head snapped up. Her eyes were red but laser-focused.

"No, I mean. She was in the bar. She looked like she could barely walk. Then she got up and stormed out like she'd suddenly gotten possessed. She came back around a half hour later looking like she'd fallen down the stairs."

"Right," Maureen sighed. "Yeah. She... she overdid it. I keep telling her that healing takes time. She thinks the second she feels kind of okay, she can do whatever she wants. She could have set her recovery back months with this little stunt."

Whitney said, "I'm sorry. I should have stopped her."

Maureen laughed. "Yeah. That would have been a shit show. Best you stood back and just let her be an idiot." She raised her wrist to look at the watch strapped there. It really was an actual watch, not the time on her phone or a fitness tracker that looked like a cyborg attachment. For some reason, Whitney really liked that about her. "I should let you get to sleep. It's really late."

"Oh," Whitney said, stepping out of Maureen's way. "It's okay. I'm used to late nights."

"Me too," Maureen said with a tired smile. "But that doesn't make it any less rude to inflict it on someone else. Have a good night."

"You too, Maureen." She watched her open the door and start to head down. She could have just let her go, but instead she blurted, "Are you sleeping in your car?"

Maureen turned. "What?"

"I... I saw your car. Downstairs, just now. It looks like you've been sleeping in it."

She saw Maureen consider lying, and saw her change her mind. "Yeah."

Whitney gestured vaguely at Catriona's apartment. "It's not the biggest place in the world, but given the rent you're paying..."

Maureen laughed. "She doesn't do roommates. And especially not if it's me. You don't have to worry about me. I'm used to it. I've actually slept in worse places."

"Well..." She couldn't just send someone down to sleep in a damn car. "My apartment isn't much bigger than hers, but there's a couch and a bathroom. Air conditioning. I don't mind sharing the space if it means you don't have to go back down there. It's not a very safe neighborhood, and it's freezing out."

"I don't..." Maureen looked down the stairs. She drummed her fingers on the doorknob. "Sleeping in a car really sucks."

"I can't imagine. Have you been sleeping there this entire time?"

Maureen shook her head. "Sometimes I found other places for a day or two. But mostly the car. Moving it around so it doesn't get towed."

"Damn," Whitney said. "Well, it'll be good until morning, and you won't get slapped with any vagrancy fines or whatever the cops do when they actually come around."

Maureen actually smiled at that. "Okay. Let me go down and get some stuff."

"I'll leave the door open for you."

"Thank you."

"No problem."

Maureen went downstairs, Whitney went back to her apartment. She left the door ajar and did a quick scan to make sure there weren't any messes or anything embarrassing laying out. A little bit of pot smell had lingered from her joint earlier, but she doubted Maureen would care about that. She straightened the couch cushions, moved the junk mail she'd tossed there earlier, and was trying to remember if she had any spare bedding when Maureen arrived.

She knocked on the door frame with her elbow, since her arms were wrapped around a sloppily-folded blanket and pillow.

"Hey. Come on in." She gestured at the couch. "It's not the Hilton or anything, but hopefully you'll think it's a step up."

"Definitely." She put her things down and looked around the apartment. "Bathroom..."

"Oh, through there. Just like the other apartment. Towels and stuff are under the sink."

Maureen nodded and made her way over. She pulled off her cap, causing thick layers of red hair to erupt from underneath.

"I'm going to go on to bed," Whitney said, retrieving her laptop. She tucked it under her arm in a way that she hoped looked casual and normal. "Don't worry about making too much noise or anything. I can sleep through a lot."

"I'll still try to keep it down."

Whitney nodded her thanks. "Okay, well. Goodnight."

"Goodnight."

Whitney went into her bedroom and shut the door. A minute or so later, she heard the shower start running. It had been a long time since she'd heard someone else moving around in her space. It was strange to be in her bed while a relative stranger was naked on the other side of the wall.

"Don't think about her being naked," she scolded herself, shifting to lay under the covers.

She fell asleep to the sound of the water running and woke to silence. She had to use the bathroom. But going would require going into the living room where Maureen was sleeping. Awkward. But the longer she thought about it, the more undeniable the need became, so she finally got out of bed and moved to the door as silently as possible on the balls of her feet.

She cracked the door and peeked out. A lamp was still on by the couch, probably some kind of makeshift nightlight. She didn't hear anything, so she assumed Maureen was asleep.

Whitney ducked out, went into the bathroom, and tried to be as quiet as possible before she flushed and ruined her chances at escaping unheard. She washed her hands, dabbed them on the towel, and opened the door to find Maureen lurking just over the threshold. It was possibly the most terrifying thing she'd ever seen and she jumped back several steps, clapping a hand against her chest.

"Shit!"

"Did you google Catriona Hendrix tonight?"

Whitney was still trying to get her heart under control. "What?"

Maureen came into the bathroom, closing the distance between them. Her face was cold, emotionless, and her voice was full of barely contained anger.

"Did you search her name online?"

"Y-yes. I was... I was curious."

"Was it the first time?"

"Yes."

Maureen held the stare so long that Whitney started to be afraid for her safety. Had she invited a psychopath into her home? Were they both crazy? Whitney's mind recovered enough for her to remember she'd taken her laptop into her bedroom.

"How did you even know I did it?"

Maureen turned and stalked out of the bathroom. Once the threat was eliminated, Whitney felt some of her bravado returning. She followed Maureen into the living room. Maureen was already back at the couch, where she snatched up a cell phone that was encased in some kind of black metal shell. It looked like it had been assimilated by the Borg from Star Trek. Maureen had to stretch her fingers out just to hold it, and the light cast a haunting blue glow on her face as she poked the screen.

"I have an alert set to catch that sort of thing so I can bury it. I get a time and a location. I was too distracted to check earlier when Catriona called. Damn it. Hopefully no one picked up on it before I could scrub the search."

"I didn't find anything, if that's what you're worried about."

"It doesn't matter. You searched for it. That means you're *aware* of her name. God, if she hadn't pulled this idiotic prank, I would just move her somewhere else to be safe."

Whitney was surprisingly panicked by that suggestion. "If anyone comes looking, I remember our deal. I won't give them your names."

Maureen gave her a quick, tight smile. "It wouldn't matter. They wouldn't take your word for it."

"Look, I may not know everything about who you are or where you came from, but I'm willing to help. If I can keep the bad guys from sniffing around~"

Maureen laughed. It was a flat, almost ugly sound. "The bad guys."

Whitney rolled her eyes. "I know, it sounds childish. But~"

"That's not what I was laughing at." She finally looked away from her screen. "I'm laughing because the people I'm worried about showing up here are cops. The government. CIA, FBI, that sort of thing. Those are the people Catriona and I are hiding from."

Whitney was stunned. "Why?"

"Because in this story, *we* are the bad guys."

INTERLUDE

CATRIONA WAS *dead.* Maureen had no doubts about that. There was no scenario where she could be in the cold for this long without being dead.

Maureen had spent the past week in a haze. They had contingency plans, they had escape routes in place, things established and tested to ensure that they would be ready when this day came. Maureen was grateful for that foresight, because it allowed her to turn off her brain and go through the motions. Step one was to trash the Hub, don't leave anything that could be recovered. Physically destroy any hardware. Hammers. Water. Fire. Leave behind nothing but slag.

Once the hardware was destroyed, the building was next. Targeted explosives, structural damage, three floors of building crashing down on the place they'd called home for the past few years. It was precise enough that only the most obsessed investigator would think it was suspicious.

Then take your go-bag and get the fuck out. Out of the city, out of the state, out of the country, if possible. There was enough money in the untraceable accounts to get her anywhere in the world. If she moved fast enough, she could vanish and start over somewhere else as someone else.

This was the step Maureen failed at.

Because even though it was clear something was wrong, and she had no doubt they were doomed, she couldn't just walk away without knowing. She couldn't leave Catriona's fate as a big question mark for the rest of her life.

So she slagged the Hub, she pancaked the building, she put some distance between herself and her normal bubbles, but then she found a place to lie low and do some digging. It wasn't easy to cut through privacy firewalls, but it also wasn't as difficult as the average person liked to believe. Her computer ran hot, literally, humming and sometimes it left marks on the table underneath it, but the pirated programs she ran were worth the risk of scalding.

She knew Catriona's contact on the job was Seaver. She didn't bother getting in touch with them, she simply dug into their financials and discovered a very large deposit of cash a few days before Catriona was called up. Maureen dug deeper into the contact's computer and found enough ammunition to counter the pay-off, then sent Seaver an email.

"tell me who paid you or everything I found goes public."

She attached one of the worst photos to the email and sent it off. Then she waited.

The reply came six hours later. "Go to hell."

She sent two more pictures, then found Seaver's private contact list and sent a few pictures to them. More waiting.

This time it was only half an hour before she got a reply. "Who the hell is this?"

"Your employer is next." She added the company's email address and a photo of Seaver's boss that she'd gotten from the official website.

Finally she got what she wanted. "I never got a name. Just a routing number."

Maureen smiled and whispered, "That's all I need."

The routing number led to a fake identity, which led to a dummy corporation, which led to a person who had never been born. But they still existed. Names and bank accounts didn't just manifest. So she dug deeper. She followed breadcrumbs. She pried away every layer until she got the name of a real breathing person.

Otis Woodward. He was a nobody, but that was to be expected. He was just a paper doll used to give a pulse to all the fake identities being used. He led her to an employer, which led her to a list of properties, which she was able to narrow down to the general area where she knew Catriona had been when she vanished. There was only one option: an abandoned high school.

At first she dismissed it as a ridiculous choice. But once she started eliminating the other possibilities, the more sense it made. School shootings had turned the buildings into veritable fortresses. The doors were nearly unbreakable, with heavy duty locks. The interior walls were very likely brick or some other thick material. And once the school was closed, the entire campus would have been closed up behind fences to prevent vandals from getting in.

Maureen arrived at the location after a day of careful travel, making sure her real name didn't show up on any manifests and passing as few security cameras as possible. When she arrived, she spent an afternoon watching the neighborhood for signs of life. There was no way to guess how many people were inside the school, but she could tell they were there. She saw one man come outside for a smoke break, and a quick jog past the former student parking lot gave her a chance to peek into a dumpster. She found lots of bloody bandages, takeout food wrappers, empty bottles of water, and other evidence that the building was occupied.

Maureen had two options. She could find a way to flush them out, or she could just go in and deal with whoever she found.

She didn't like guns, but she knew how to use them. And they were incredibly effective at this sort of thing. She had no doubt she could've come up with a clever plan, given the time, but Catriona had already been prisoner long enough.

In the end, she was surprised to find there were only four men inside. She briefly wondered if one of them was the person she'd used to track down the location, but she couldn't remember if his name had been Otis or Otto. It probably didn't matter. They were just there to keep an eye on things. Hired guns, eyes to look for suspicious behavior, large bodies to dissuade normal people from getting too close. They weren't the men hurting Catriona.

She killed the first man when he came out for his smoke break. She had scaled the fence the night before, using the cover of darkness, and hid under the dumpster until everyone was inside. Then she waited by the door with the most cigarette butts scattered around it and waited. When the smoker came out, she shot him in the back of the head and grabbed the door before it could close behind him.

The second man was whistling as he wandered the halls. Maureen hid in a nook and, when he was close enough, stepped out and used three bullets on him. Chest, chest, head. She had a silencer, but the gunfire was still loud in the tiled hall, echoing off the rusted lockers. She stepped around him and headed back the direction he'd come.

They had set up a monitoring station in what she assumed had once been some kind of Theatre classroom. Six televisions showed different angles of Catriona in a featureless room, strapped to a chair, her body slumped to the side. An empty chair positioned in front of the screens was still spinning, propelled by the person who had just been seated there jumping up, so

Maureen ducked as she entered. A bullet chipped the door above her head, and she fired toward the sound of it. She hit the man in his thigh. He tried to fire again as he went down, but the shot went wild. She eliminated him with another headshot.

She found a map on the door showing the fastest route to the parking lot in case of a fire and used it to determine the most likely place for Catriona to be held.

"Are you one of her contacts?"

The fourth man's voice echoed too much for her to tell where it was coming from. She stepped into the doorway and listened carefully.

"I'm just a substitute," she said. "I'm supposed to be filling in for Mrs. Glickman."

He actually chuckled. "I know where her classroom is. Why don't you come here and I'll walk you there."

"Sure thing. Just tell me where you are."

"Tell me where you're starting from."

Maureen chuckled and leaned against the door frame. "I guess they don't tend to hire idiots, huh?"

"I guess not," the fourth man said.

She closed her eyes and let the weariness creep into her voice. "I don't want to kill you, man. I don't... I don't like hurting people. Honestly, I'm probably going to cry myself to sleep tonight thinking about these guys I just killed. Did... did they have families?"

"Not really." The fourth man was getting closer. "The one with the mustache, his name is Ike. He had a kid, but I don't think he sees her much. Even less now."

"Shit," she said under her breath.

"Tell me where you are," he said, his tone placating and almost comforting. "We can work something out. You don't want to kill me, I don't feel like killing anyone, either. I'm just supposed to watch the place, you know? I don't know what the hell is going on half the time. I just wanted the paycheck. So I think we can figure a way out of this without anyone else getting hurt. Okay?"

"I'm in a big room with a bunch of TVs," she said.

She moved away from the door. She grabbed the collar of the man she'd killed, dragged him across the floor, and propped him up against the wall. She took off her jacket and draped it over him, then moved deeper into the room.

A few seconds later, she saw a shadow in the hall. As soon as she saw it, the corpse by the door was hit by two more bullets.

The fourth man stepped into the doorway and looked down at his *former friend.* "Ah, shit, Eddie…"

Maureen tried to shoot him in the head, but her position was awkward. It threw off her aim, and she hit him in the throat. He still went down, instinct making him drop his gun to use his prominent hand to stop the blood. Her second shot was more accurate and he collapsed on top of his friend. Maureen exhaled and came out from hiding.

"I might still cry," she assured him. "Crying over four bodies isn't much different than crying over three."

She crouched next to the men and patted them down. She swore when she didn't find any keys, which forced her to backtrack. She found the keys on the second man, so she thanked him and hurried deeper into the school.

Her destination was a music room next to the cafeteria. The walls on either side were shared with classrooms, which implied heavy soundproofing. And it was centrally located, meaning there were no windows. The main classroom had five separate practice rooms branching off of it, and she found Catriona in the center room.

Maureen crouched next to the chair, unsure if it was safe to touch her anywhere. Her face was painted with blood, and wiping it away only revealed bruised skin underneath. There was a cut along her hairline which had been sutured in what looked like a professional manner. One eye was swollen shut, and the white of the other eye was disturbingly red. Three of the fingers on her right hand were splinted.

"Hendrix?"

Catriona flinched, then recognized her voice and tried to lift her head. "Reena."

"Don't worry about the guards. I took care of them." She risked touching one hand. "What did they do to you?"

Catriona grunted. Her head dropped back down.

"Can you walk?"

There was no response, so Maureen pulled out her knife to start cutting away the restraints. She'd been prepared to carry Catriona out of here if she had to, and it was definitely looking like it would be necessary. She just hoped they didn't run into the next shift of guards on their way out.

"Don't worry, Hendrix," Maureen said as she lifted the other woman up. The battered body was dead weight against her side, but she braced herself and started walking. "I'm going to find somewhere you can get better… somewhere safe they won't find us."

Catriona mumbled something incomprehensible.

"Just let me worry about that," Maureen said. "I've got you. For right now, I've got you."

CHAPTER FOUR

"SO Y..." She felt acid starting to boil up in her throat so she stopped, took a few deep breaths, and then tried to speak again. "You're criminals?"

"Nothing pedestrian, don't worry." Maureen sat down on the couch, still poking at her phone. Her eyes darted from side to side as she read something on the screen. "We're not staking out a bank or planning to rob you or anything. We aren't petty thieves."

Whitney moved into the living room, giving the couch a wide berth. "So what kind of criminals are you?"

"The kind people like you would normally never have to think about."

"The kind who kill people?"

Maureen didn't hesitate. "Yes."

"Have *you* killed~"

"Yes." She finally looked up from her phone and locked eyes with Whitney. "I can't tell you how many. And I can't tell you they all deserved it. A lot of them probably didn't. Is that going to be a problem?"

Whitney was shaking and wrapped her arms around herself to keep Maureen from noticing. "You just told me you're a murderer and you ask me if that's a *problem*."

"Not a murderer. A killer. There's a difference."

"What on *Earth* could be the difference?"

Maureen sighed and lowered her phone. "Think of it like a quarterback tackling someone during the Super Bowl. That's just part of the game. But that same player tackling someone in a bar, that would be awful. That's the difference between killing and murdering."

"You just compared it to a game."

"Sometimes that's how I think of it." She brought the phone up again.

"What the hell are you doing on that thing?"

Maureen grunted. "I'm trying to make sure your little Google search didn't send up a thousand flares for the people looking for us. And I'm trying to do it in a way that won't let them know I'm looking. It's an extremely delicate process, and talking to you at the same time is not helping. Can I please spend five minutes on this and then I'll answer all your questions. Okay?"

Whitney nodded. It would give her time to put her thoughts in order. She went to the kitchen and filled a glass of water, drank it all, then filled it again. When she finished the second glass, she went back into the living room. She turned on a lamp and sat in an armchair, watching Maureen tap, type, and swipe on her phone screen.

She looked different now. Her eyes were harder. Her hair was still a wild mess, but now it made her look almost deranged.

Finally she tossed the phone onto the couch, closed her eyes, and pinched the bridge of her nose.

"We got lucky. It doesn't look like anyone picked up on your search. But you cannot do that again, understand? You won't find anything, anyway."

"Okay. So can you answer some of my questions?"

Maureen exhaled and rubbed her hands over her face. She had long fingers, slender, and her thumbs bent back at the second knuckle in an odd way that almost made them look inhuman.

"Catriona was an asset for an organization. Before you ask me to be more specific, I can't. They worked for the government, our government, but they won't have a name you'd recognize. They don't have the fancy offices with a view of the National Mall. She worked in a basement. Cinder blocks, no windows, really bleak stuff. But that's the kind of agency it was, and it was the work they did.

"Catriona was what they called a fixer. If a problem cropped up somewhere in the world, she took care of it. Presidential candidate we don't like getting a little too much support? Guerilla army getting a little too cocky about not wanting our help? Officials balking at the terms of some contract we're about to sign? Catriona went in and found a way to ease things back onto the right path."

Whitney said, "By murdering someone?"

"Sometimes. It didn't always require assassination. Blackmail worked, too. Sometimes all she had to do was show up in someone's house and that was enough to scare them onto the straight and narrow."

"So who were you?"

Maureen got up and went to the kitchen. She poured herself a glass of water before she answered. "I was her God's eye," she said, sitting on the couch again. "We were in contact whenever she went into the field. I hacked into satellites and surveillance feeds so I could tell her exactly what she was walking into. I made sure she got in safe and got out in one piece."

Whitney was holding her glass with both hands, watching the water to make sure she wasn't still shaking. "You said you worked for our government. But you also said they're the ones you're hiding from."

Maureen sneered and leaned back. "The woman who was in charge of the agency disappeared. It happens sometimes in this business, so things were just shuffled around. New management. The new guy in charge didn't like that his most effective agent was a woman, so he decided to clean house. Bring in his own crew. Unfortunately, Catriona always expected a rainy day. She was prepared. All her files, her contacts, even her reports were hidden away in a place the new guy couldn't find them. A lockbox they could never find or break into."

"I guess that's how she ended up like this."

"New Boss tried to torture it out of her. I actually have no idea how he managed to capture her, or exactly how long she was held prisoner before I found her. But he tortured her the entire time. He had doctors on-hand to fix whatever he broke, then let her heal just enough so he could break her again. But he only broke her physically. Never mentally."

Whitney said, "She never gave up her contacts or the, the other stuff? How do you know?"

Maureen took a long drink, then shrugged. "Because no one ever showed up to drill into my brain."

Whitney blinked. "You're the lockbox?"

"Catriona never wrote anything down if she could help it, and she certainly didn't have a typed list of people who owed her favors. She told me. I remembered."

"That's kind of amazing."

Maureen didn't react; she just stared straight ahead at the shared wall between the apartments. "I got her out," Maureen said. "Then I got as far as I possibly could and tried to bury her somewhere they'd never find her so she could heal, and then we'd figure out the next step together. And then she has to go out and assault some penny-ante goons. God, what the hell was she thinking."

"They run a protection racket," Whitney said. "They take a thousand dollars a month from me, and probably as much from a half-dozen other places around the neighborhood. All in the name of keeping us safe." She scoffed. "Not that it helps. We've still gotten robbed a half dozen times since they started extorting me. But it's better than the alternative."

"Is it?" Maureen said.

Whitney started to answer, stopped, then pushed a hand through her hair. She slumped back into her chair. "I honestly don't know. But it's *easier* than the alternative."

Maureen nodded. "That, I'll buy."

They sat in silence. Whitney wasn't sure what time it was, but she doubted she would be able to get back to sleep following everything she'd just heard.

"We can be gone by morning."

Whitney looked at Maureen. "I don't know if that's what I want."

Maureen raised an eyebrow. "I just told you we're killers."

"Yeah, but you..." She gestured. "You're just playing the game. And I'm not in the game. None of my customers are in the game. So no one will be in danger. Except you and Catriona, if I turn you out in the cold. And while it might have been misguided, she was only trying to help me tonight. And honestly, your cash has been a godsend. That kind of money doesn't come from a saint who runs charities on the weekend. Part of me knew it had to be blood money, and I took it anyway. I'd be a hypocrite to kick you out now just because I know all the details. Well, most of the details. The pertinent information."

"Thank you," Maureen said. "I'll do my best to make sure she keeps her head down from now on."

"I'd certainly appreciate it." She stood up and pushed her hands into her hair. "I'm going to take a shower and then try to figure out how to spend the rest of the morning."

"You're not going back to sleep? The bar just closed a couple of hours ago."

"You expect me to sleep after all of this? I know you probably don't have a problem shutting down your brain, but I lead a much more boring life than you."

Maureen smiled and sat up straighter. "Okay. Go lie down. Breathe in for four seconds. Hold your breath for seven seconds, then exhale for eight seconds. Do it over and over again. And while you're doing it, tell yourself to stay awake. Insist on it. Demand it. Tell yourself you *must* stay awake for another hour. You'll be out in no time."

Whitney raised an eyebrow. "That works? Reverse psychology on myself?"

Maureen shrugged. "I've slept on a helicopter sitting between two people with shoot-on-sight orders against them. I think you'll be okay."

"I'll give it a shot."

"Good luck."

Whitney went back into her bedroom and laid down on top of the blankets. Her mind was racing with what she'd just learned. She knew she should've been terrified. She shouldn't even stay in the apartment. She should run downstairs, call the police, and have them take the killers away. But something made her hesitate. Some twitch at the back of her brain. Was she scared of Maureen? Not really. She was a little scared of Catriona, but at this point the woman seemed to consider Whitney a friend. Calling the cops would make her an enemy, and she *really* did not want to become Catriona's enemy.

She tried Maureen's breathing trick. It wasn't going to work. She'd tried breathing exercises in the past. Her brain wasn't the kind that would just shut off because she told it to. And insisting on staying awake another hour? She was definitely still going to be awake in an hour. She was kind of looking forward to it. She could go out there and rub Maureen's smug face in just how poorly the advice had...

"Just let me do the talking," Bridgeman muttered as they entered the office.

The three men shuffling behind him like whipped dogs didn't say anything. The blood had been washed away, but bruises were starting to bloom all over their exposed skin. Josh looked the worst of them all. He was completely soaked, and the water had been shallow enough that he hit mud when he landed. It dislodged something in his back, and he lurched with every step like Quasimodo. Bridgeman's entire right hand was throbbing, and he could barely move the fingers. Definitely not a good sign. But he could wait to get it looked at. They had much more important business to take care of first.

Everything in the office was built for intimidation. The walls were lined with dark-stained shelves filled to the brim with leatherbound books whose titles were too faded to read in the dim light. The carpet was forest green and so thick that they could have stomped into the room without making a sound. The two guest chairs were so large and blocky that, even with the cushions, they reminded Bridgeman of electric chairs. The desk looked almost seaworthy, and at the moment its shining surface was cleared of everything except a handful of ledgers.

The man behind the desk sat in a chair that looked like a throne. Two tall windows on either side of him showed the sherbet-colored glow of dawn. It cast their host in shadow but that only made him scarier, more mythological.

Krikor "Koko" Ohanian was sitting back in the throne, fingers laced over his stomach, regarding them with an unblinking stare. His chin was jutted out to deepen his frown.

When Bridgeman was next to the chair, Ohanian lifted his hand just enough to make a "Sit" gesture. Bridgeman didn't hesitate. His three companions remained standing; none of them had been invited to take the other seat, and none wanted to take the unofficial second-in-command position. Ohanian stared at them as if taking note of this reluctance and filing it away for later. Then he pushed himself up and leaned forward.

"What happened."

Bridgeman swallowed. "We got carried away at the strip club. We were just fooling around. One of the girls was acting kind of flirty with David. We-we just got carried away."

Ohanian held his stare on Bridgeman with no emotion in his face. Bridgeman tried not to fidget. They'd decided on this version of events on their long walk following the attack. They couldn't tell the truth. Couldn't tell Ohanian that some masked asshole had gotten the best of them all. And then he only stole one envelope? That was insult to injury. Bridgeman decided he was going to take care of the masked squirt by himself. But that meant he needed an explanation for why he and his boys looked like ground beef.

"The bouncer pulled David off her," Bridgeman said. "Colin shoved the bouncer. Then some other employees got involved, and we all sort of got into it."

Bridgeman had told the strip club manager he could either back up their story, or they could make it the truth by roughing up his employees. He'd eagerly agreed to call Ohanian and report their 'bad behavior,' leaving out the part about how they'd shown up already looking like they'd gone ten rounds.

Ohanian leaned back in his chair like a throne. "Money."

Bridgeman had put all the envelopes into a canvas bank bag, which had been hanging off Colin's shoulder. Colin pulled it off and placed it reverently on the desk. They'd pooled their own money to replace the envelope which had been taken; a thousand bucks from some dive called the Whipjack. Barely anything, especially cut four ways, but he seethed at the principle of it.

Ohanian didn't move to take the bag. He looked at each of the men in turn, lips pursed.

"Why is he wet?" he asked, pointing at Josh.

"A whole tray of beer got dumped on him."

The menacing man considered that. "Which one of you is David?"

David sheepishly lifted his hand.

Ohanian heaved himself up out of his chair. The office had been built to cater to his impressive size but he still loomed over them as he came around the desk. He was six-foot-eight, three hundred pounds, and Bridgeman imagined he could feel the ground shake with each step. He stopped in front of David and stared down at him. David, trembling, looked up to meet their employer's gaze.

Ohanian punched him in the side of the head.

Since the large man's fist and his employee's head were roughly the same size, it was a horrific blow even at such close distance. David dropped like his strings had been cut, folding in a pile at Ohanian's feet. Ohanian drew one of his legs back and then swung his tailored shoe into David's gut as hard as he could. David's body jerked and bounced back a few inches. Ohanian kicked him again, then again, moving each time David shifted. After he was done kicking, breathing heavily from the minimal exertion, Ohanian gestured at Bridgeman.

"Lay one of his hands flat on the floor."

"What?" Bridgeman said.

"Do it, or it'll be one of yours."

Bridgeman got out of his chair and knelt next to David. He grabbed one of his arms. David fought him, but Bridgeman knew there was no stopping what was about to happen. He forced David's hand down onto the carpet and held his wrist tightly. He wanted to squeeze his eyes closed or turn his head away, but he knew if he did, Ohanian would only order him to watch. So he looked, but he kept his eyes unfocused.

"Don't fuck with my business again, David," Ohanian said.

Then he brought his foot down on the back of David's hand.

CHAPTER FIVE

WHITNEY WOKE up aware there was a murderer in her apartment. There were three people in the building, and two of them had taken lives.

Strangely, the thought came with a feeling of calm. She didn't know how many other criminals were in the area. Thieves, rapists, murderers. Catriona and Maureen were the devils she knew. And they definitely seemed like nice devils. They'd bulked up her bank account beautifully, and Catriona had apparently put her health at risk to get the protection money back from Bridgeman. However ill-advised the stunt had been, she couldn't deny it had been done with the intention of being helpful.

She got out of bed and put on a robe before she peeked out into the living room. The couch faced away from her room, but she got the sense that the apartment was empty. She quickly gathered her things and moved to the bathroom to take a shower. She lingered under the spray, using it as an opportunity to shut out the rest of the world and focus on her thoughts.

Maureen was a killer. Catriona was a killer, although that was a much less startling revelation. They were fugitives from justice. Potentially terrorists, since the government was after them. The money that had saved her life was, without a doubt, blood money. Payment for assassinations or some other dark assignment. But if she started moralizing about where her customers got their cash, in this part of town, she might as well just close shop.

She liked Maureen. She didn't know if she liked Catriona, but the woman had obviously been through hell. And Maureen was sleeping in her car! Whitney couldn't kick them out if it meant they'd essentially be homeless. It didn't matter what kind of people they were. Knowingly doing that would make *her* the monster.

Whitney shut off the shower and combed her hair back out of her face and wrapped herself in a towel. She dripped in front of the sink to brush her teeth, staring into her eyes to see if there was any doubt in them. She looked pretty confident, so she pushed aside her misgivings.

She opened the bathroom door to find Maureen standing directly across the threshold. Whitney jumped back and clutched at her towel.

"Jesus, stop doing that!"

"Sorry." Maureen's eyes darted down, toward Whitney's bare shoulders and upper chest. They might have lingered before she averted her gaze toward the window. "I just wanted to tell you that I... got you breakfast. It's just, um, McDonalds. But I thought it might be a nice gesture. As a thank you for letting me stay here."

"Oh." Whitney's hair and fallen into her face when she jumped, and she smoothed it back down. "I-I usually don't wake up before they stop serving breakfast."

"It might have to be heated up. But that's the level of cooking I'm comfortable with."

Whitney managed a smile at that. "I do appreciate it. Thank you. I just... let me..." She nodded toward her bedroom.

"Yes, of course." She stepped back and let Whitney slip past. "There's one more thing."

Whitney looked back. "Good or bad?"

Maureen furrowed her brow, still keeping her eyes focused on anything that wasn't Whitney or her towel. "I guess that depends. Catriona wants to meet you."

"We sort of met last night."

"True. But she wants to talk."

Whitney raised an eyebrow. "Oh really. Well, that's good. Because I want to talk with her, too."

Maureen exhaled sharply. "Don't say that until you've actually had a conversation with the woman. I'll warm up your McMuffin while you're getting ready."

"Thank you."

Whitney closed her bedroom door, trying not to let her mind focus on Maureen's ominous warning. No matter what happened, this is what she'd been hoping for since she first caught a glimpse of her mysterious tenant. They were actually going to sit down and talk. She would just consider anything awkward, scary, or uncomfortable part of the rent. She opened her closet and looked at the options available to her.

What *does* a person wear to a meeting with a government assassin...?

Whitney ate her breakfast - had McMuffins always been so delicious? - and then followed Maureen down the hall to the other apartment. Maureen knocked and then opened the door without waiting for a response. Whitney remained in the hall like a child terrified of entering her parents' bedroom. Maureen looked back at her and motioned her inside. Whitney took one last breath of free air, braced herself for whatever was about to happen, and stepped over the threshold.

The apartment was almost entirely unchanged from the last time Whitney had been in it, when she showed it to Maureen all those weeks ago. It smelled a little like a hospital room; antiseptic and that ineffable chemical smell of medicine and salves that created a sort of fog that lingered near the ceiling. She saw a trio of trash bags near the sink, all full and tied off.

Catriona was sitting in the armchair facing the door. She was wearing a black hoodie and blue jeans. It was the first time Whitney had seen her without something obscuring her face. Her hair was dark brown and seemed to have been sloppily cut into a manageable length, probably by Maureen if she hadn't done it herself. The skin under her eyes seemed bruised, and a mostly-healed break ran along the bridge of her nose. Catriona's eyes had locked onto her as soon as she came into the apartment, but it didn't feel like an ordinary stare. It was like one of those paintings where the eyes seem to follow you around the room.

"Catriona Hendrix," Maureen said, then swept an arm toward Whitney. "Meet Whitney Mercer."

"She told you everything?" Catriona's voice was surprisingly strong, but there was a wavering under the consonants that betrayed her true weakness.

Whitney glanced at Maureen. "I guess. She told me who you

are and wh-why you need a place to lie low. She told me you're not exactly the good guys."

"I guess it depends on where you're standing."

"I guess it does," Whitney agreed. "What did you do last night?"

Catriona squared her shoulders and finally looked away. "I followed those young men to the bridge. I made sure they knew I was there. One of them hung back to intimidate me, and I threw him into the river. I'm fairly sure he survived the fall, but I admit I didn't confirm it. When his friends came back to check on him, I disabled them and retrieved your money."

"Disabled how?"

"It wasn't difficult. One blow each. They aren't fighters."

Whitney sighed. "Well, I'm sure that will be comforting when they come back and destroy my windows and release rats in my kitchen. They don't have to be fighters to get revenge."

"They're cowards. Once they've been challenged~"

"You think they haven't been challenged before? People have refused to pay. I'm sure you saw the empty storefronts all up and down the street. Dumpsters mysteriously catch fire. Deliveries accidentally get misdirected. Your employees are mugged every time they get within ten feet of your front door."

Catriona took a deep breath. "Oh."

"I don't want to sound unappreciative. I know you were trying to help. But these guys won't just go away on their own."

"So we make them go away."

"We..." Whitney looked at Maureen, who had retreated back to lean against the wall. She was hugging herself, and just shrugged at Whitney's unspoken question. She turned to Catriona again. "What exactly do you mean?"

Catriona just looked at her.

"You're not going to kill them."

"Why not? It would be easy."

Whitney almost laughed. "You can't... you can't just kill people."

Catriona seemed confused. "They're a menace. They've ruined the livelihoods of people trying to work in this neighborhood. They're parasites."

"I can't believe I'm standing here explaining why you can't kill Bridgeman."

"It does seem odd," Maureen said.

Whitney tossed her an annoyed look. "No one needs to die. They should be arrested."

"That would require evidence that they're behind all the harassment you've attributed to them," Catriona said. "And even if you got lucky and they were arrested, put on trial, and convicted, how long do you think it would be before they were out and ready for retaliation?"

Maureen said, "And they're obviously not self-employed. They're just the pick-up men. If you stick them in a cage, whoever the real boss is will just get some new recruits to take their place."

"Won't the same thing happen if you kill them?"

Maureen shrugged. "Harder to fill a position if it's empty because the last guy doing the job was murdered."

Whitney put her fingers against her forehead and massaged. "This isn't real. I'm not really talking about murdering Bridgeman. I want to be crystal clear that it is *not* happening. It's not your fight. You're just renting this apartment. You have nothing to do with my business or the decisions I make about running it. If I think paying the protection money is worth it, then you just accept that and keep your mouth shut. Is that clear?"

Catriona looked at Maureen, then flipped her hand up. "I won't interfere."

"Thank you." Whitney put her hands together. "As for everything else, you can stay here as long as you need. You've basically paid for a year of rent upfront, so I'm not going to put you out on the street. I don't know if I agree with everything you've done. But hell, I don't know if I disagree with it, either. As long as I don't know many details I can just give you the benefit of the doubt. So I'm going to go with that, and just say you're welcome to stay as long as you want. But no more interfering with things, okay? We'll just stay in our neutral corners."

Catriona glanced at Maureen, then lifted her hand and dipped her chin. Whitney took that as an agreement.

"Good. Oh, and obviously you're welcome in the bar any time. And with the money you've already given me, you can go ahead and consider your tab comped for as long as you're here."

"I appreciate that. The biscuit was good."

Whitney nodded. "Thank you." She looked at Maureen. "That goes for you, too. We serve food. I want to be sure you're eating well."

Maureen raised her eyebrows, surprised to be included in the conversation. "Oh. Thanks."

Catriona said, "Are you sure you don't want to ask any questions about~"

"No! Nope." Whitney held her hands up as if blocking her from saying anything else. "The less I know, the better. Ignorance is bliss in this case. You seem like nice enough people, and until I actually need to know more, I'd rather just move on."

"Works for me," Catriona said. "It was good to finally meet you."

"You, too."

Maureen pushed away from the wall and walked Whitney back out into the hallway. She closed the door quietly behind her.

"That was amazing," Maureen said softly once they were alone. "I don't think I've ever heard her say that much to anyone until she knew them for six months."

Whitney shrugged. "I'm a people person."

"Apparently," Maureen said.

"I meant what I said about the food. I know you just got breakfast, but if you want a late lunch, or dinner. Or a midnight snack."

"Thanks. I might take you up on that tonight."

Whitney glanced at the apartment door, then looked back at Maureen. "You knew that I tried to search Catriona. Did you search me?"

"I did. I had to make sure you were trustworthy."

"I guess I passed muster."

"To be honest, there wasn't a lot to find. No social media. A few articles about the Whipjack, but mostly involving times you were robbed or vandalized."

Whitney winced. "Not the greatest way to make the papers."

"There are worse ways." Maureen let that comment hang in the air, then shifted her weight from one foot to the other. "There was also... something... about your mother."

Whitney tensed. "How... how'd you find that? I... w-we didn't have the same name."

Maureen squinted one eye closed and tilted her head. Whitney sighed.

"Right. Of course. Why would something as trivial as that get in your way?"

Her mother, Charlotte Marchand, had been the original owner of the Whipjack. It was her dream, and she had been planning it since before Whitney was born. She finally opened it when Whitney was ten. Every dime, every spare minute was spent trying to keep the place alive. Whitney did her homework at the far end of the bar while her mother served drinks. It had a rough start, but by the time Whitney was in high school, there was a light at the end of the tunnel. It was turning a profit. It was getting good foot traffic. It looked like it was on the verge of becoming a success.

And then one morning, Charlotte didn't wake up. Whitney knew she'd been taking pills to stay awake, but she didn't know where they came from or even what they were. That night, Charlotte had taken too many, and she washed them down with a few too many beers.

The cause of death was obviously an overdose. The police had been very careful talking around her, but it didn't take long for her to learn manner of death was suicide, not accident.

Whitney cleared her throat and pushed the memories away. "It wasn't a suicide."

"I don't have an opinion," Maureen said. "I just thought it was right to tell you that I knew. It doesn't seem like the sort of knowledge a person should have unless it's given to them, and you deserved to be aware that I knew."

"Oh. Okay. Thank you. Any other skeletons in my closet you dug up?"

"No, I don't know anything about your father. Except for the fact that if your mother was French, he must have been... ah..."

"Chinese," Whitney said.

"Right. So that's all I know about him."

Whitney sighed. "Join the club. If you do happen to dredge anything up about the guy, I wouldn't mind hearing it."

"Noted." She looked toward the stairs. "So what happens now?"

"I don't know. What do you usually do all day?"

She almost saw the wall drop down over Maureen's face. "I drive around. I find wi-fi hotspots and I do... research."

Whitney knew she wouldn't get any more information out of her, and she felt too exhausted to try. "Well, I spend this time prepping to open the bar. You're free to hang out and see that glamorous life if you want. The bar does have wi-fi, and at least this way you won't have to worry about the owner running you out for not buying anything."

Maureen smiled. "That actually sounds pretty nice. I'll take you up on that."

They moved toward the stairs. "And if you get bored, I can always put you to work washing dishes."

"How well does that pay?"

"We'll start you out as an apprentice. Sleeping on my couch is your wage."

Maureen laughed. "Sounds fair. Lead the way, boss."

Bridgeman's broken wrist was fucking killing him. He'd gone to a doctor on Ohanian's payroll, a guy so deep in shit that he could be trusted not to report four guys who'd clearly been beaten up. David had been fog-brained after hitting his head on the pavement, and getting his hand crushed under their boss' shoe had rendered him completely useless. He was at home now, resting, hopped up on painkillers. Bridgeman wished he was home, too. Drunk or medicated enough to forget how much his wrist hurt. But there was unfinished business in South Park.

He hated that he'd lost the fight. Hell, he couldn't even call it a fight. They'd walked up to that punk and he'd thrown three punches, and they went down like high schoolers. It was humiliating. He needed to make amends if he was ever going to show his face around here again.

Bridgeman was currently parked on the corner where he usually started his monthly rounds. A pharmacy on one corner with a garage across the street. Neither of them were pickups, but maybe someone who worked there had taken offense to Ohanian's protection services. Maybe some hero decided to act before Bridgeman came knocking.

He opened the truck door and climbed out, cradling his right hand against his side as he started walking. He was going to retrace his route, visit all his usual friends, and one of them was going to give away their involvement. Ohanian would never have to know what really happened, and anyone who got the bright idea to do a repeat performance would receive a valuable lesson.

No one messed with Peter Bridgeman and got away with it.

CHAPTER SIX

WHITNEY LIKED having Maureen in the bar while she prepped for the day. She took a seat in the same booth Catriona had the night before, but she brought her phone and laptop with her. She found a charger and plugged them both in, then began typing rapidly. She was too involved with whatever work she was doing to chat, and Whitney had her own tasks to perform, but just having another person present was a nice change of pace.

Whitney was about to suggest making them something for lunch when the bell over the front door chimed. She sighed and made a mental note to start locking the door until they opened. She started to say they were closed but the words died when she saw Bridgeman strolling toward the bar. He was currently looking toward Maureen, so she had a few extra seconds to compose herself before he turned his attention to her. She pressed her lips together, swallowed the lump in her throat, and acted like she would if this was any other day.

"We're closed. And I thought part of our deal was that you only dropped by once a month."

"Maybe I want to check the place out. See what makes it so popular that you can afford our prices." He climbed onto a stool. Whitney noticed his right wrist was in a brace, the knuckles of that hand alarmingly purple. He looked back at Maureen again.

"Besides, how can you be closed if you've got a customer?"

Whitney said, "She's a friend. She's using the wi-fi." She thought of the recovered envelope of cash she'd put next to the register. Had she moved it? Was it out of sight? If it was there, if he noticed it, would he recognize its significance?

"I'm a friend. Can I just use a stool? I've been walking a lot today. Got a lot of people to talk to."

She ran through a list of reasons to tell him to get the hell out, but none of them seemed strong enough. And she knew that the harder she fought, the harder he would dig his heels in.

"Fine. Just don't bother me, okay?"

"I'd love a glass of water, when you get a second."

She rolled her eyes and went into the kitchen.

***

Maureen hated the guy on sight, and her feeling was magnified when she realized he was the guy scamming Whitney. And if this was the guy, then Catriona was responsible for that nasty looking paw of his. She still thought it was an insanely stupid thing for her to have done, but she had to bite back a smile at the sight of the damage. Just from this brief introduction to him, she could tell he deserved this and infinitely worse.

Whitney left to get his water, or more likely to just put a wall between her and this asshole, he immediately slid off the stool and sauntered across the room to her booth. She resisted the urge to swear out loud and instead focused on her screen.

"Hi there."

She cut her eyes up toward him. She flashed the quickest of smiles, then looked away.

"I'm Pete. Pete Bridgeman. Has your friend ever mentioned me?"

"No."

He chuckled and rested his left hand on the back of the other side of the booth, tilting his head toward her.

"This is the point where you tell me your name."

"Is it?"

He chuckled and sat down across from her. Maureen minimized the window she'd been using and opened a new one. She started typing.

"You get a lot farther in life by being friendly," he said. "All you have to do is give me a name, so I can refer to you by name, which makes things a lot nicer. More polite. It would allow us to have a conversation."

"Since not telling you my name is a hindrance to that, I feel like I'm made the correct choice."

Bridgeman snorted and shook his head. "It's just a name, girlie. I'm not asking for your social security number."

Maureen recited a nine-number sequence that started with 535. Bridgeman's brow furrowed and he sat up straighter.

"Wait, that's..."

"Yours," Maureen said. "At least that's the social security number for Peter Adam Bridgeman, thirty-two years old, born in Cle Elum, Washington. Parents are Gregory and Kathleen Bridgeman."

The color had faded from his face. "How'd you know that?"

"You gave me your name," Maureen said. "I'm showing you it's not as harmless as you claim. In the wrong hands, a name can do all kinds of damage. I could destroy your credit right now. Hell, give me an afternoon, and I could erase you. So I don't think I'm going to be giving you my name any time soon, Peter Adam Bridgeman, and I would prefer if you returned to your seat at the bar. I have a lot of work to get done, and you're distracting me."

He stared at her, mouth agape and brows still twisted in confusion. Maureen stared back at him, expressionless.

Whitney came out of the kitchen with a glass of water. She looked at the empty seat where Bridgeman had been, then pivoted to see where he had ended up.

"What's going on?"

"I'm explaining to Peter why he can't know my name," Maureen said. "I just demonstrated to him that names can be dangerous things."

"Okay..." Whitney approached cautiously.

Bridgeman had recovered somewhat, and he narrowed his eyes at Maureen. "Were you here last night? I'm almost positive I remember someone sitting in this booth. Was that you?"

"I was nowhere near this place last night," Maureen said.

He glared at her. She returned his stare without blinking. Her face was a complete blank, idyllic. She blinked once, a signal that she wasn't going to engage in a childish staring contest with him. But she also wasn't going to look away.

Whitney said, "You asked for some water."

"Sure," Bridgeman muttered. He slid out of the booth, took the glass, and looked down at Maureen. He faked like he was going to spill the glass over the laptop. She didn't flinch, didn't even pull her hands away from the keyboard. She just stared up at him with the same smile, the same blank eyes, and waited. He grimaced, looked at Whitney, turned away from them both. He slammed the glass down on the bar hard enough to splash water on his hand, which he shook dry as he went to the door.

"I'll see you in a month, Mercer."

"I'll be dreading every minute."

She took the water back behind the bar and dumped it in the sink. Maureen watched her, looked toward the door to make sure Bridgeman actually left, then slid out of the booth.

"I'm starting to understand why Catriona went after the guy."

"The master of first impressions," Whitney said, scrubbing the glass even though he'd never taken a drink. "What did you do to spook him so much?"

Maureen shrugged. "He said there was no harm in giving him my name. I proved that was wrong by looking him up. People get very antsy if you recite their social security number at them."

Whitney looked at her, raising her eyebrows. "Damn. That's pretty evil."

"I wanted him to know who he was dealing with. Someone like that, you can find basic stuff under the first layer of the onion. I'm used to digging a lot deeper for people who actually make the effort to be invisible. It's the same thing as you looking up something on Amazon."

"Hopefully it was enough to scare him away until the next pickup."

Maureen was surprised. "You're still going to pay him the protection money?"

Whitney shrugged. "Yes. I explained all this upstairs. It's cheaper than the alternative. Besides, he's obviously going around trying to find out who beat up him and his guys last night. If I suddenly stop paying, he's going to know I was involved. I don't want him sniffing around here any more than he already is. I don't think Catriona wants that, either."

"You're right," Maureen admitted. "But it also sucks that he's just getting away with it. How much money do you think he gathers every month from the places around here?"

"No idea. But he's nice enough to have a sliding scale depending on income. He only extorts a little more than what people can comfortably afford."

"What a peach." She drummed her fingers on the counter, looked back at her equipment, and decided it was a good time to take a break. "I'm going to go do some errands. If I grab lunch while I'm out, do you want me to get you something?"

"Uh, sure. Yeah."

"It might be a while." She retrieved her phone. "Give me your number and I'll text you when I know where I'm going to stop."

They exchanged numbers and Maureen closed her laptop, putting it behind the bar where Whitney could keep an eye on it. Maureen promised she would be back as soon as she could, then left the bar.

On the sidewalk, she tucked her hair under her cap, buttoned her coat up to her chin, and stuck her hands in her pocket. She could still see Bridgeman at the far end of the street. She waited to give him a good lead, then turned and started following him on his route.

Bridgeman never looked behind him. It was an odd, and borderline stupid, move for someone who had been ambushed on this route just a few hours earlier. It only proved what she'd already deduced; he wasn't the brains behind the operation. She still took precautions because she *was* a professional at this sort of thing. She would hate herself forever if this imbecile happened to catch her just because she'd been sloppy.

He wasn't spending much time at each stop, which meant he wasn't doing a thorough investigation. She figured he was just showing his face and expected the owners to be scared into a spontaneous confession. Stupid, sloppy, time-wasting.

She followed him northeast through South Park and waited whenever he went into a business. At the bridge, he actually did slow and take a look around the area. Did he think whoever attacked them lived under it? Maybe there was a troll they'd neglected to pay for crossing. He must have figured out that whoever had hit them came from one of the earlier stops, because he didn't bother crossing the bridge. Maureen ducked into a recessed doorway until he passed - he never even turned his head toward her - and then continued her pursuit.

He ended up about a mile south of the Whipjack, where she watched him get behind the wheel of a truck and speed off. She tapped the license plate number into her phone and ran a quick search. She didn't get the name of any stops he might make on the other side of the bridge, but she figured her list was complete enough to do something with it.

She stopped at an Indian restaurant she'd noticed during her walk. She got lunch for her and Whitney, then returned to the Whipjack.

"He's got a pretty fat client list," Maureen said as she put the food down on the bar.

"What?" Whitney peeked into one of the containers. "Who?"

"Bridgeman. I followed him. I figured he was hitting up every place where his attacker might have come from."

Whitney's eyes widened. "That was incredibly dangerous."

"It would have been, if the guy had any awareness of his surroundings. I could have walked down the middle of the street humming a tune and he never would have picked up on it. He's a dummy."

"That doesn't make him harmless."

"Of course not. In a lot of ways, it makes him a lot more dangerous. But it does tell me he's not the head honcho." She took out her phone and saw the search had yielded results. "A protection racket is child's play, but you need *some* intelligence to pull it off successfully. He's just the hammer."

"So who is swinging him?"

Maureen read the results off her phone. "His truck is owned by someone named Krikor Ohanian. Ring a bell?"

"Krikor?" Whitney laughed. "Is he a wizard?"

"It's, um..." She thought for a second. "Armenian, I think."

"No, I don't know any Armenians. Definitely no one named Krikor."

Maureen shrugged and made a note. "I figure if he's paying for Bridgeman's truck, he's most likely the one getting reports."

"Huh." Whitney had brought silverware out of the kitchen and placed a set in front of Maureen. "Do you think he told this Ohanian guy about what happened?"

"Doubtful. If the big boss thought he'd been robbed, he would strike back hard. But his foot soldier is out here all by himself. Bridgeman must have told some lie about how they all got hurt, and he's trying to restore his dignity by making amends."

Whitney said, "I guess that makes sense. Thank you for the food, by the way. This is from Lucknow?"

Maureen nodded and mumbled "mm-hmm" around a mouthful of chicken korma.

"Excellent choice," Whitney confirmed. "How much do I owe you?"

"You can get the next one."

Whitney sighed and stirred her Chana masala. "I'll just add it to your rent for using the couch."

Maureen chuckled. "Works for me."

They ate in silence, Maureen seated at the bar and Whitney standing on the other side. At one point Whitney disappeared into the kitchen and came back with two bottles of beer. Maureen took hers gratefully and took a long drink.

"You know," she said when she put the bottle down, "if you change your mind about Catriona doing something about this mess..."

Whitney waved her hand to cut off the rest of whatever she was about to say. "I don't know what you're actually offering, and I'd like to stop thinking about it before I'm forced to understand. We're nowhere near... whatever she would do. Okay?"

Maureen held up her hands in surrender. "You're the boss, boss."

"I'm sure you have better things to do." Whitney nodded toward the shelf where Maureen had stowed the laptop. "Whatever you've been using that thing for seems pretty complicated, given how much you were typing. You were able to find everything you needed on Bridgeman in a couple of seconds."

Maureen chuckled. "Hacking him was like breaking into a sixth grader's laptop. I'm surprised his password wasn't Password. The people I'm looking for..." She worked her jaw from side to side and looked into space past Whitney's shoulder. "It's like finding a needle in a haystack, but the haystack is behind six firewalls, and you have no idea where it is. There are a lot of layers to peel back, and there's no guarantee I'm even going down the right road until I find something useful or hit a dead end and have to start over."

"Sounds frustrating. But I'm sure it takes up enough of your time. I don't want you going after Bridgeman."

Maureen shrugged. "The offer is on the table."

"Thanks. Seriously. Thank you."

Maureen smiled at her, then went back to her lunch. She knew Whitney wanted to be a good person, the kind of person who wouldn't set someone like Catriona Hendrix after her enemies. But she also knew people like Bridgeman only tended to get worse over time.

Soon enough, Whitney would have to make a hard choice, and Maureen would be waiting.

For now, she was just going to enjoy her food.

CHAPTER SEVEN

BRIDGEMAN FOLLOWED Ohanian's assistant down the foreboding hallway to the terrifying man's office. He told himself the summons had nothing to do with what happened on the bridge. It had been almost a month and there hadn't been any fallout. His wrist was healing, and Colin and Josh were also both on the mend. David was still at home, but his hand had gotten pretty well mangled by Ohanian's stomping session. Bridgeman did feel a little bad about that, but it was a small price to pay to really sell their version of events.

He hated that he still had no idea who was responsible for the beatdown. He'd gone back to South Park six times since that night. He dropped in on people, showed up in the middle of the day or right at closing. None of them seemed guilty. They were still scared of him. Anyone with a pit bull in their back pocket would puff up and act like a big man. He didn't see that in anyone on the route. He thought it was kind of suspicious the guy had only taken the money from the Whipjack, but it had been the last stop. So maybe the guy thought that was the only envelope they had. It could also have just been a misdirect, something to make him *think* the Whipjack was the place to focus on. He was too clever for that.

So who the hell was the dude in the mask? Where'd he come from? Bridgeman worried he was starting to mix up what really happened with fake memories. Originally he thought the guy was little, but hadn't he been the same size as Colin? And he was definitely wearing a full black facemask, right? Or maybe just a regular ski mask, with glasses over it? The more he thought about it, the more the guy transformed into a comic book villain.

Ohanian was writing something when the assistant stopped in front of his desk. "Mr. Bridgeman is here to see you, as requested."

The assistant left without waiting for a response. Ohanian didn't look up, but gestured at the chairs with his free hand. Bridgeman sat.

A clock ticked. He listened to the sound of pen on paper and looked past Ohanian at the curtains covering the window just behind him. Finally Ohanian put down the pen and looked up at him.

"Your friend David is dead."

Bridgeman blinked. "What?"

"The head injury. There was a bleed."

"God. When did it hap~"

"I sent a man to the strip club so the person responsible could be dealt with appropriately."

Bridgeman's blood chilled.

"It took some convincing before the manager admitted that he was lying." Ohanian's eyes bore into him like a drill. His voice was absolutely calm, like a breeze over a frozen lake, and it was far more frightening than if he was shouting. "He said he was lying for *you*. He said he hadn't seen you at all that night until you walked in looking like shit warmed over. So I want you to tell me, right now, what actually happened that night."

David decided there was no point in trying to continue the lie at this point. "I'm not exactly sure. I've been trying to find out, but~"

"What. Happened."

Bridgeman pressed his lips together. He shifted in his seat. "We were on the bridge, o-on the way out of South Park. Josh had spotted someone following us. He went back to suggest, uh, to tell them to take a hike. I don't know what happened, but Josh ended up in the river. The rest of us went back to find him, and the dude was~"

"What 'dude'?"

"I don't know, sir. I've been trying to find out all month." Ohanian motioned for him to continue. "He was just standing there. He went nuts on us. Kicked all our asses. We-we got in a few licks of our own, of course we did, but the guy had... a pipe. And I think he was wearing a helmet. Hitting him in the head hurt us more than it hurt him. We didn't stand a chance."

Ohanian leaned back. "Your hands were fine."

"What?"

"No scraped knuckles. No sign you'd thrown any punches at all, let alone punching a helmet. You didn't fight back at all, did you?"

Bridgeman decided not to say anything.

Ohanian sighed and folded his hands over his stomach. "You've been trying to find this man. I assume you haven't had any luck."

"No, sir."

"Then *try harder*. Those people pay for protection? Take it from them until they give up whoever this masked man is. Choose one place and burn it to the fucking ground. Then make sure the others know why it happened. Then burn another one, and another one, until they stop fucking around and give up the asshole." He watched Bridgeman and then, raising his voice for the first time, shouted, "Go."

Bridgeman leapt up from his seat and hurried out of the room, face burning. Despite all his threats and posturing, he didn't really want to destroy anyone's business. They'd broken windows before, caused a little mayhem, but to actually burn a place down? It was a lot.

But he would do it. Risking the wrath of Ohanian was not worth preserving some stupid laundromat or motel. He straightened the collar of his shirt and slowed his pace as he left the building. He already had a list of viable candidates. His next pickup was in three days.

Sometime in the next forty-eight hours, someone in South Park would burn.

Whitney had never had a roommate before. She was a little worried when the days became a week that she and Maureen would start getting on each other's nerves, but the opposite happened. They adjusted to one another's routines. Maureen bought groceries and cooked so many meals that soon Whitney's fridge looked like a shelf at the supermarket. Lunch became a series of impossible choices, none of them bad. Maureen switched to Whitney's sleep schedule so they would be awake at the same times, and she started hanging out in the bar while Whitney was working.

Two or three weeks into the new arrangement, while they were alone in the kitchen, Violet finally commented on it.

"So is she some kind of tech... person...?"

"Who?" Whitney asked. They were both in the kitchen prepping for the first rush of the night.

"Your girlfriend."

Whitney laughed. A little too loudly, she thought, but it was too late to compensate. "What do you mean? I don't have a... no. I'm not... wait, do you mean Reena?"

Violet raised an eyebrow. "You call her Reena?"

"It's her name. Her nickname. It's... wh-whatever, it's what she told me to call her. That doesn't make her my girlf- we're friends. She needed a place to stay and I had space available."

"Okay," Violet said, sounding as if she'd been convinced of the exact opposite.

Whitney hoped she wasn't blushing. "And to answer your question, no. She's... I don't know exactly what she is. But it involves her phone and her laptop and a lot of typing."

"Probably something with Amazon," Violet guessed. "Everything is Amazon these days."

"Yeah," Whitney said.

The truth was that she still hadn't learned much beyond what Maureen had told her that first night. She and Catriona were bad people who did bad things for a Certain Government Agency. She knew Maureen was a decent cook, and didn't mind making dinner after Whitney had spent all night making burgers and fries for customers at the bar. She didn't like music but didn't mind if Whitney listened to it at her normal volume. Once she'd even caught Maureen humming a Radiation Canary song while she was doing her mysterious work on the laptop.

Catriona, however, was as much a cypher as ever. Everything she knew came second hand from Maureen, as Whitney hadn't spoken to her tenant since they were introduced. She was still recovering. As Maureen warned, her stunt on the bridge had set her back a few weeks.

It was the night before Bridgeman was due to pick up his monthly payments. Whitney couldn't help wondering if it would be business as usual or if he'd have extra protection. When she closed up the bar for the night, she made sure the locks were secure and the bars had been pulled down over the front windows before heading upstairs.

Maureen had gone up ahead of her and was just getting out of the shower. She had changed into sweatpants and a T-shirt, her damp hair combed back out of her face.

"Hey," she said. "Do you want something to eat? I was about to fix something before bed."

Whitney hadn't had time to stop for lunch. "Sure. Nothing too heavy, though."

"Definitely not," Maureen agreed, going into the kitchen to examine the options.

Whitney changed into pajamas in her bedroom and came out to find Maureen microwaving Chinese that was leftover from the day before.

"I decided to be lazy," Maureen explained as she took the boxes from the microwave.

"Don't call my original plan lazy," Whitney said, taking a seat on the couch.

Maureen got silverware and brought the food over. She sat across from Whitney, pulling her feet up onto the cushion and turning to face her.

"I think this is the first time I've seen you without a phone or a computer within reach," Whitney said.

"Wait, what?" Maureen looked around, feigning panic. "Oh god, oh no..."

"Jerk," Whitney said. "Try to give a lady a compliment."

Maureen grinned and poked at her food. "I feel safer with the connection. It's like someone with bad vision trying to drive without their glasses. Without the phone, I know there's so much there I'm missing. Stuff I won't be able to see. It might be dangerous."

"It's right over there on the counter if you want to grab it."

"That's okay," Maureen said. "I feel safe here."

Whitney was surprisingly touched by that, but she covered her smile by popping a piece of chicken into her mouth. "So..." She finished chewing before she continued. "I can understand how Catriona could get into this kind of business. I don't know anything about her, but I can't exactly see her working as a mechanic."

Maureen had just taken a bite and pressed the back of her hand against her mouth as she laughed.

"Why aren't you working in some computer company? You've

clearly got the skills. You could be... hell, I don't know what kind of computer jobs there are. You could be doing a Google on Amazon. You could make a billion bitcoins. Why are you spending your time picking up groceries for a scary-ass government operative?"

"Because tech jobs are boring as hell. And I didn't want to make billions, let alone become a Zuckerberg. I may have caused some damage in my life, but I tried to only hurt people who deserved it. I'm not selling anyone's personal info, or targeting grandmas with misinformation about the president. And I..." She looked into her takeout box and pushed rice around with her fork.

"I get it," Whitney said softly after a minute. "Sorry. I didn't mean to pry."

"No, you're fine. I just haven't really talked to anyone about this." She pushed her hair out of her face again. It was starting to dry, frizzing a little. "When I was ten, my mother got really sick. It hit her so fast, just out of the blue. Huntington's. I was all she had, so when she started to decline, it was up to me to take care of her. Eventually it was easier to stop trying to juggle school with being her caretaker and I dropped out. I could find pretty much everything I needed online anyway.

"So I spent the next few years going between taking care of Mom and learning how the internet works. It was like walking around a neighborhood over and over again, until you knew who left their doors unlocked when they went to work and which backyards had a pool you could use. I knew how to get things, find things, unlock secrets. I unlocked the wrong door, or the right one, and someone found me. They asked if I needed a job but I said I wasn't interested. He left a card anyway. Told me to be in touch. So when Mom passed away, and I didn't have anything left, I gave them a call."

Whitney raised an eyebrow. "I guess that explains why you're so comfortable taking care of Catriona, too."

Maureen smiled. "I've always taken care of her. When she was on missions, I was the angel on her shoulder. I kept her safe. I like to think I kept her sane. Or as sane as she ever was. There were other handlers at the agency who treated their operatives like video game characters. Unplug from the machine for a break, go about your day, don't spare a thought for the person on the other end of the line. I never forgot Catriona was out there somewhere. She was alone. And even if she didn't *feel* alone, as she told me many times, I like to think she appreciated knowing I was there if she needed me."

"It's a great feeling, to be someone's touchstone."

"Mm-hmm," Maureen admitted. She reached out with one bare foot and bumped it against Whitney's leg. "What about you? Parents."

Whitney sighed. "I guess in a way it's not much different from your story, except I'm still taking care of my mother's sickness. This bar strangled her to death, and I'm here keeping it alive because... I don't even know why. It's a job, and I need a job, and it's something I know I'm good at. And staying is easier than finding something new and starting over."

"Oh," Maureen said. "I'm sorry. I didn't mean to open any old wounds..."

"You didn't. Honestly. I've made my peace with it. I had to, or else I would've gone crazy by now. It's not a bad life. I provide a service. I make people happy. There aren't a lot of jobs where you can say that. I'm lucky to have this place and call it my own."

Maureen nodded. "It's a nice bar."

"Thank you. Even if it was a sensitive subject, it's been so long since I've talked to anyone like this, I think the pangs would be worth it. I like talking to you, Reena."

"Same."

Whitney took another bite of her food. She thought maybe some chicken had gotten burnt, and used her fork to search for the blackened piece. She had almost given up when Maureen suddenly twisted to look toward the kitchen.

"Does it smell like something's burning...?"

Whitney was off the couch and moving to the window before Maureen had finished asking the question. She heard Maureen follow her, and they crowded together to look out at the street. Whitney was terrified the smell had been drifting up from the Whipjack, but was shamefully relieved to see the light of flames reflected on buildings to the north.

"Can you tell what's burning?" Maureen asked.

Whitney started to shake her head, but then she checked the corners. "Damn, I think it's Kaiser's Pizza. I loved their deep dish."

"That's one of the places on Bridgeman's list."

"Are you~ of course you're sure. Damn it. And there's no way this is a coincidence."

Maureen backed away from the window. "This is my fault."

"The hell it is," Whitney said, returning to the couch for her phone. "You didn't tell Catriona to go after them. Something like this was going to happen eventually no matter what she did."

"Should we go down there?"

Whitney could already hear sirens on the block, so she canceled the call. "I don't know what that would accomplish. We'd just be getting in the firefighters' way. Besides, Bridgeman is probably down there somewhere watching. He'll want to see us all shivering and scared in our pajamas. We won't give him that satisfaction."

They both went back to the window and looked out. The firefighters were already at work, and the flames seem to have been beaten back quite a bit. But even with the quick response, it was clear that the pizzeria was likely a lost cause. Whitney alternated between watching the spectacle and scanning the street. Other people had come out on the sidewalk, wrapped in robes and their hair mussed from sleep. She wondered how many of them had come to the same conclusion, how many saw this fire for exactly what it was: a warning.

"Should you go downstairs and check on the bar?" Maureen asked. "He might be making his way down the list."

"No. He wouldn't do multiple places in one night, especially not with the fire department already on the scene. This was a message to everyone else. He'll make sure we hear about it when he comes by for his money tomorrow night."

Maureen sighed. "I'm sorry."

"It's not your fault."

"I know. But I'm still sorry this is what you have to deal with just to run a business."

Whitney shrugged. "Cost of doing business. If I moved somewhere else, I'd probably be paying a lot more than a thousand dollars in extra rent." She scratched her eyebrow and started for the bedroom. "I'm going to bed."

"Okay. I hope I didn't keep you up too late."

"No." She looked at the couch and stopped. She turned to face Maureen. "Do you want to share my bed?"

Maureen's eyes widened. "What?"

"You've been on this couch for weeks. Don't tell me it's comfortable after I just spent all this time sitting on it. You deserve to spend at least one night in a real bed."

"I don't know."

"The offer stands, if you change your mind."

She was almost to the bedroom door when Maureen said, "I'm

gay."

Whitney looked back. "Okay."

"I just... wanted to tell you that, in case it had any bearing on whether or not you were willing to share the bed with me. It might make some people awkward."

"We're both grownups," Whitney said. "It's not that big a deal."

Maureen sighed. "Okay. Then I think I will take you up on it."

"Great."

Whitney went into the bedroom and left the door open. She rearranged the pillows as Maureen turned out the living room lights, eventually coming to join her.

"Door open or...?"

"Doesn't really matter," Whitney said.

"Right."

She left it ajar, glanced to see which side of the bed Whitney seemed to be choosing, and went to the other side. Whitney half expected her to stay on top of the blankets, or maybe build a wall of pillows between them like kids on a sleepover, but she slid under the covers with only the slightest hesitation. She sighed as she settled in on the mattress.

"Oh, wow. Yeah. This is definitely a step up."

Whitney smiled. "I'm glad you approve. I never really thought about how shitty the couch must be for you every night."

"The only nice thing I can say is that it's better than my car. Damning with faint praise, I think they call that."

"Yeah," Whitney chuckled. "If you ever want to sneak up here and take a nap while I'm at work, that would be okay with me."

"Thanks." She had her hands folded on top of the blankets. "Thank you for being so nice to me. I'm not... really... used to nice."

Whitney turned her head on the pillow to look at her. "Catriona isn't constantly showering you with compliments?"

Maureen laughed. It was a loud, spontaneous sound, and it made Whitney smile. "Not so much. Doing well is expected, so unworthy of commenting on."

"Seems like a peach."

"She's a good person. Well, maybe not a good..." She sighed and rubbed her fingers across her eyes. "She doesn't have anyone. I mean, no one. She never has. I'm the first person who has ever been there for her. The first person she's ever counted on. That means something to her. Maybe the average person can't see it, but I can."

"That's all that matters," Whitney said. "I'm glad she has you."

Maureen was quiet for so long Whitney thought she'd fallen asleep. But then, in a very small voice, she said, "Thank you, Whitney."

"You're welcome."

She stared at the ceiling until she heard Maureen's breathing become still and steady. She turned her head toward the window. The curtains usually reflected a streetlight's glow, but tonight it was combined with the red-and-golden strobing lights from the fire engine. They had gotten lucky that Bridgeman hadn't chosen the Whipjack. She felt horrible for thinking it. The Kaisers were good people, and they didn't deserve to be used as an example like this. The pizzeria was their livelihood. She couldn't imagine what they were going to do without it.

She turned her head to look at Maureen, fast asleep next to her. She was a bad person, and she admitted she was directly responsible for multiple deaths, but right now... she was at peace. If she could do awful things for a living and still sleep like this, then maybe Whitney could afford having one bad thing on her record. Maybe, if it was for a good cause.

Just in case, she pulled the blankets up and rolled onto her side. She should try to get as much quality sleep as possible before she unleashed the hounds.

CHAPTER EIGHT

THE PIZZERIA was a total loss. Whitney walked down the street to get coffee, using the trip as an excuse to get a close-up look at the damage. It was horrifying. The entire front of the building was a burnt cinder. All the windows were shattered, and she saw twisted stools and mangled tables within. One side of the menu, which had hung over the passthrough to the kitchen, had fallen and crashed onto the countertop like a giant axe blade.

The article she'd found online said the fire chief believed it started in one of the ovens. At the moment they weren't ruling out foul play, but initial inspection made them believe it was just faulty equipment. Whitney didn't know if that was better or worse. It depended on how well Bridgeman covered his tracks and what kind of insurance the Kaisers had, she supposed.

When she got back to the bar, Maureen was sitting in what had quickly become her usual booth. She had her hair loose, parted on the left so the majority of it gathered on her right shoulder like a big bolt of red cotton. It had been strange waking up next to her. They'd been facing each other, and Maureen's eyes were already open when Whitney first looked at her, but she saw them flicker into focus so she was pretty sure the other woman hadn't been staring. They'd exchanged quiet good mornings before they got out of bed and went about their separate routines.

Maureen looked up now as Whitney slid into the booth across from her. Whitney put down one of the coffees in front of Maureen, who picked it up and inhaled the steam before she took a sip.

"How did the place look?"

"Awful. Completely ruined. There's no way Kaiser is going to be able to fix it up and start over. They're ruined."

Maureen shook her head.

"I want to do something."

"Like?" Maureen asked.

Whitney shrugged. "I can't just say I want..." She held up her hand, miming a gun. "But Bridgeman is obviously prepared to step up his game. The only other option is to sit here and wait for him to burn someone else's business down. I can't cross my fingers and hope it isn't me next time, because eventually it will be. Something has to be done. And if you and Catriona are willing, I'm not going to stand in the way for some moral high ground."

Maureen held up her phone. "I can send her a text right now. But if I tell her you're okay with it, I can't guarantee you can call her off later. You have to be sure."

"For the Kaisers," Whitney said. "And for whoever gets targeted next. I can be okay for them."

"Okay." Maureen lowered the phone and sent the text. "He's coming by tonight for the monthly payment, right?"

Whitney nodded. "If he keeps to his schedule."

"Do you need any help with that?"

"No, thanks." Whitney smiled. "Catriona's rent is due, though, so you can decide how much you want to pay this month."

Maureen said, "Well, I *am* using two apartments now..."

"Eh. One and a half."

A few minutes later, the door to the interior stairs opened and Catriona limped out. She still looked rough, but her recuperation seemed to be going along nicely. She was dressed in black jeans and a black T-shirt, her hair pinned back sloppily. She scanned the room as she came around the bar and slid into the booth next to Maureen.

"You're certain?"

Whitney nodded. "He's escalating. Someone could have gotten killed last night. If drastic measures have to be taken to prevent that, I'm okay with whatever happens to him."

"Stopping Bridgeman might not change anything. If we get rid of him, the man in charge might just pull someone else from his stable. Someone worse."

"I know. We'll have to take that chance."

Catriona looked at Maureen, and something passed silently between them.

"What she's saying," Maureen said, "is that for anything real to change, she needs to go after this Ohanian guy."

"I can't ask her to do that."

"You'd rather ask me to do a half-assed job? The kitchen is flooding, Miss Mercer, and you just want me to run a squeegee over the floor a couple of times. The water will come back if you don't stop the leak."

Whitney pressed her lips together. "I didn't know I was asking you to do something so big. Ohanian sounds like a... like a big deal."

"He's not," Catriona said with confidence.

"He has his own army of goons."

"Who are terrorizing a tiny little square of a Seattle suburb. He's a tin king with a paper crown. I've taken down people who would have made Ohanian wet his pants. I just want to make sure you're okay with going that far."

Whitney thought about the Kaisers. Either of them could have been at the restaurant late, either to do the books or maybe cleaning up after a late shift. They had two kids who could've been there.

"Go as far as you need. The people of this neighborhood have been paying for protection for long enough without getting anything in return. They deserve to finally feel safe."

Catriona nodded once and got up.

"Where are you going?" Whitney asked.

"Recon. I got lucky last time. I want to know what I'm walking into."

Maureen was already out of the booth. "Wait, hold on. I'm not sure that's the greatest idea."

Catriona turned and faced her. "I have to get out of the apartment sometime. And if the people looking for me have gotten this far, it's only a matter of time before they close the noose anyway." She started toward the exit again. "I'll keep my eyes open for spotters. If they get me, they get me."

"I don't like that philosophy," Maureen shouted after her.

Catriona just lifted a hand over her shoulder as a farewell gesture as she stepped out into the sunshine.

Whitney looked up at Maureen. "What are the chances she's actually in danger out there?"

"Probably low," Maureen admitted with a sigh. "She's right. If the people we're hiding from knew she was in South Park, they would also have the address."

"Can I just ask again, exactly how worried should I be about that happening?"

"There's an extremely good chance I'll know they're coming well before they're close enough to strike. So we'll leave before that happens, and the worst that will happen to you is a relatively short interrogation. They might try to scare you by putting you in a windowless room, but they don't have the authority to actually hurt you. Hell, they don't have the authority to withhold food or water. Torture's definitely off the table."

"That's not exactly as comforting as you seem to think it is."

Maureen sat down again. "You'll be fine."

"You're not worried I'll crack under pressure and give you away?"

"No, because you won't have anything to give away. One day we'll just be gone and you won't have any idea where we went. I'm giving you permission now, tell them whatever you know. Don't try to protect us and get yourself hurt."

Whitney was surprised by how shocked she was by that. She'd always known that was the endgame of their arrangement. But she'd accepted that and filed it away before she'd really gotten to know Maureen. Before they'd shared a bed and talked over late-night meals.

"You wouldn't even say goodbye?"

Maureen caught the subtext in Whitney's voice and looked up. When she spoke again, there was an extra touch of tenderness in her own voice.

"No. I would say goodbye."

"Good."

Maureen smiled and looked at her laptop screen again.

Whitney called Violet and told her to take the night off. She didn't know what to expect when Bridgeman showed up, but she didn't want the girl to be caught in the middle of what might be a dangerous situation. When Catriona hadn't returned by nightfall, she looked at Maureen to see if they should worry. Maureen caught the glance and shook her head.

"She's hunting. I wouldn't expect her back until morning, and that will just be for a change of clothes and maybe shower. She's been locked in a box for a long time. I would be surprised if she came back a second earlier than absolutely necessary."

"As long as you're not concerned."

"Borderline," Maureen admitted. "I'm used to being in her ear when she's out in the field. But she can handle herself, even if she hasn't been at a hundred percent for a while. She's tough. Resilient."

Whitney nodded and focused on her work to keep from worrying. It worked well enough that when the bell chimed a little after ten-thirty, she was surprised to look up and see Bridgeman walking up to the bar. She tensed and glanced at Maureen before she went to the cash register. Bridgeman followed her gaze and wrinkled his nose when he saw her.

"Nice to see you have regulars," he said. "They hide the fact that you never have any real customers."

"Can we do this without the banter for once?" Whitney took the envelope out of the money tray and dropped it in front of him. "We already heard from you once this month, and that's enough for a lifetime."

"Still so rude? Even after what happened to the pizzeria?"

Whitney raised an eyebrow, fixing her expression to be as bored as possible. "Why would that change anything? It was just an accident, right? If it was sabotage, it would mean your protection services were basically useless. I know the Kaisers were paid up, because they were one of the busiest places on the street."

Bridgeman pursed his lips and took the envelope off the bar. "Yeah, about that. We really took a hit, losing them. So if we want to break even, we're going to have to raise everyone else's fee. You know what it's like with a business. Always gotta cover costs. The new price is fifteen hundred a month."

Whitney bristled. "That's ridiculous."

He shrugged. "You could always cancel your service. What's life without a little risk, huh?"

"Bastard." Whitney put her hands on the bar and hung her head. "Fine."

"Fantastic." He rested his elbows on the bar across from her. When she looked up, he smiled in a falsely casual manner. "Oh, the new fee starts this month."

"Bullshit," she said. "You can't just spring something like that on people."

He held out his hands, helpless. "We have bills just like everyone else. The Kaisers aren't going to be paying this month. We have to make up the shortfall. This month was especially rough." He held up his hand to show off the wrist brace. "Some of our employees have extensive hospital bills that need taken care of."

"I don't have that much cash on-hand."

Maureen slid out of the booth. "Whitney... it's okay. I can cover it."

Whitney frowned. "I can't ask you~"

"It's fine." She pulled out a pocketbook and approached cautiously, as if Bridgeman was a wild animal that might pounce at any second. "You said five hundred extra?"

Bridgeman turned to look at her fully. "Just who the hell are you, geeky girl? Little computer girl just hanging around in a bar at all hours? You like this place enough to give her that big of a tip?"

"I just don't want any problems." Maureen's voice was so quiet, Whitney could barely hear it. She held the pocketbook in her left hand, pulled the bills out with the right. She tried to count the money one-handed, but her fingers wouldn't cooperate and she dropped them. "Oh shit, oh no..."

Bridgeman crouched down to pick it up. He reached for the fallen money with his uninjured hand. Maureen swung her foot up and brought it down as hard as she could, pinning his hand to the floor. He jerked away in surprise and shock, but she was putting her full weight on the ball of her foot. She grabbed the golden rail of the bar with one hand, then kicked his wrist with her other foot as hard as she could. The snap was so loud that Whitney jumped back from the bar, eyes wide as Maureen grabbed Bridgeman's head with both hands and shoved it down. Her knee met his nose halfway, and he was rocketed backward with a spray of blood from his broken nose.

"Reena, what the hell," Whitney gasped.

Maureen sighed and adjusted the collar of her sweatshirt. "He's just a pawn. Taking him out won't change anything in the big picture. And honestly, I was just so fucking sick of hearing him talk. I don't know how you deal with him for so long."

Whitney couldn't catch her breath. She came closer and leaned over the bar to see Bridgeman was still conscious but, judging by the glaze in his eyes, had no idea what they were saying.

"What happens now?"

As if in response to her question, the front door opened and Catriona came inside. She looked at the bloody man on the floor, then at Maureen, and then at Whitney.

"What do you want me to do?" she asked.

Whitney swallowed the lead ball in her throat. "Can I leave that up to you?"

"Sure."

Catriona crouched and hooked her hands under Bridgeman's shoulders. She dragged him to the door and stopped long enough to flip the sign over to CLOSED. Whitney started to protest, but she honestly couldn't imagine serving any drinks after what she'd just seen. Bridgeman didn't fight as Catriona dragged him onto the sidewalk, dumped him, and came back to close the door behind her. She glanced at Maureen.

"You've got some blood on you."

Maureen and Whitney both looked and saw a spray of blood across her neck and the shoulder of her sweatshirt.

"The customer bathroom," Whitney said, pointing to it.

"Right," Maureen said, already tugging at the shirt as she went.

Whitney went to the door and looked outside. Catriona had gotten a car from somewhere, one that Whitney didn't recognize, and Bridgeman's body stayed limp as she hauled him up into the passenger seat. Once he was out of sight, Whitney decided she didn't want to see what the next part of the plan was. She twisted the lock and pulled down the blinds. She also turned off the overhead lights so no one would assume the sign was a mistake. She would lose a night of business, but the envelope holding her monthly payment was still on the bar, so she figured she could afford it.

She followed the sound of running water to the bathroom. Maureen was standing at the sink with her back to the door. She'd taken off her sweatshirt, revealing a sleeveless white T-shirt. Whitney stopped just outside the bathroom, arms wrapped protectively around herself as she watched Maureen scrub at the blood on her sweatshirt.

"I'm usually better at leaning back when that happens," Maureen said when she realized she was being observed.

"You didn't have to do that."

Maureen didn't say anything, but she stopped scrubbing.

"I'm glad you did. Thank you."

"You're welcome."

Whitney's mouth was suddenly dry. She was shaking as if the temperature of the bar had dropped twenty degrees since she turned out the lights. She hugged herself tighter and looked down at the floor. She saw it again in her mind. Maureen's body as she kicked. The way Bridgeman's head had snapped back. The kick. The snap of his head. She looked up and found herself transfixed by the muscles of Maureen's arms.

She took a step into the room without thinking and brought her hand up. She brushed the tip of her middle finger up the line of Maureen's bicep, holding her breath until she reached the edge of her shirt. Maureen dropped her sweatshirt into the sink basin. She looked up, and her eyes met Whitney's in the mirror.

"This happens sometimes," Maureen said, her voice even. "The shock of violence combined with the physicality of the act. If someone isn't used to seeing that kind of thing, it can create feelings that can easily be confused with sexual arousal. It's a hero thing. I came to your rescue so you're going to feel... grateful... and it's easy to confuse that for something else."

"Okay."

"Okay?" Maureen said.

"Okay, I understand what's happening," Whitney clarified. She used the back of her hand to push the hair away from Maureen's neck. She thought she felt Maureen shiver, but her fingers were trembling enough on their own that she couldn't be sure. "Does that mean I can't follow through on it?"

Maureen bit her bottom lip and looked away from the mirror. "Not necessarily."

Whitney stepped closer. She kept one hand on Maureen's shoulder and wrapped the other around her waist, pulling her close. Maureen gripped the sink with both hands. Whitney bowed her head and pressed her lips against Maureen's neck. The tension faded out of Maureen's body as Whitney sucked gently, like a teenager trying to leave a hickey. She brushed her tongue over the skin, which was already wet with warm water from being thoroughly scrubbed.

"Are you sure this is—"

"I want you fuck to me," Whitney interrupted, moving her lips up to Maureen's ear.

Maureen made a purring sound and turned in Whitney's arms, leaning back against the sink. Their lips met, and Whitney sank into the kiss, closing her eyes and letting her hands roam. Maureen seemed hesitant at first, but soon returned the kiss with equal passion, pulling away just enough to get her hands between them so she could unbutton Whitney's shirt.

"I wanted to make a move," Maureen said. "When you invited me to sleep in your bed. But I didn't... I didn't know if you meant it as an opening or..."

"I didn't," Whitney said. "But I would've welcomed it."

"Now you tell me."

"Now it's relevant."

They kissed again, and Maureen pulled Whitney's shirt off her shoulders. It fell to the ground and was quickly followed by Maureen's T-shirt. Maureen shoved off the sink and pressed herself against Whitney, walking her back until she hit the wall. Whitney allowed herself to be pinned there, lifting her arms over her head as Maureen kissed her jaw, her throat, and bent her knees to go lower. She drew an S on Whitney's chest between her collarbones and then dragged her tongue down, licking her cleavage before she kissed along the edge of Whitney's bra.

Whitney opened her eyes and looked straight ahead, seeing the reflection of them in the mirror. She kept her arms up, but clasped her hands together and dropped them down to the top of her head. Maureen kissed her nipple through her bra as her hand slid up Whitney's spine to find the clasp and undo it. Whitney dropped her arms to get the bra off and toss it aside, then laid her hands flat on top of her head again.

Maureen straightened to admire Whitney's beautiful breasts, then noticed her position. She met Whitney's gaze and slid her hands over the flexed biceps, leaning in to kiss her again. She held Whitney's wrists loosely as her other hand skimmed over her ribs, up to her breast. Whitney closed her eyes and arched her back, pressing herself into Maureen's palm. Maureen's tongue slipped over her bottom lip and then she sank down again, releasing Whitney's wrist but skimming her fingers all the way down her arm as she knelt in front of her.

Whitney looked in the mirror again. She saw herself suck in a breath when Maureen kissed her stomach, saw the tremble in her jaw when the tip of Maureen's tongue flickered against her navel. She finally dropped her hands and buried them in Maureen's hair. It was thick and heavy between her fingers as she tugged it loose. She looked down to see it explode out, falling down her back as Maureen tugged her pants down over her hips.

"Don't stop," Whitney whispered.

"I wasn't planning on it, sweetie," Maureen said, then kissed Whitney's thigh and pulled her underwear down. Whitney bent her knees and rolled her hips forward. Maureen kissed her and Whitney pressed hard against the wall to keep from falling over. She swayed and held onto Maureen's head - her hair really was so much more magnificent down - and tried to focus on what was being done to her with lips and tongue.

Whitney lost herself in the pleasure. It had been ages, not just since someone had gone down on her, but since she'd just shut off her mind and let herself feel good. She didn't even masturbate regularly, and her body felt electrified.

Maureen pulled away and wiped the back of her hand across her lips as she stood up. Whitney mumbled a half-hearted protest, but stopped when Maureen moved her to the sink. Maureen pressed up against her from behind. Whitney gripped the sink with one hand and put the other against the wall next to the mirror. Maureen put one hand between Whitney's legs and cupped her breast with the other.

"Look," Maureen said, and then began sucking Whitney's neck.

"What...?"

"Look at her."

Maureen pressed two fingers into Whitney and began to slowly thrust into her. Whitney's knees threatened to buckle, but she tightened her grip on the sink to stay up. Her fingers curled against the wall. She looked straight ahead. She could see Maureen behind her, eyes open and watching.

"Not me," Maureen said. "Look at *her*."

Whitney looked at herself. She licked her lips and fought the urge to close her eyes as Maureen started moving her hand, twisting her fingers.

"Give that pretty lady a kiss," Maureen whispered into her ear.

Whitney leaned forward, grateful that she kept a clean bathroom for her customers, and pressed her lips against her reflection. She opened her mouth and gave the glass a tentative lick. She still had her eyes open and, combined with the fact she'd just been kissing Maureen and her brain was short-circuiting from being so near orgasm, it actually did feel almost like she was kissing herself.

She only pulled back when she came, twisting her neck so she could kiss Maureen until the waves finished crashing into her.

Afterward she rested her forehead against Maureen's, eyes closed, trying to catch her breath. Maureen kissed her cheeks and eyelids, brushing the hair away from where it had gotten stuck to the sweat on her face. When her thumb brushed over Whitney's bottom lip, Whitney captured it and pressed a kiss to the pad.

"Are you okay?" Maureen asked.

Whitney opened her eyes. "Yes. Thank you. But I want more."

Maureen raised an eyebrow and smiled seductively. "There's more?"

"I said I wanted you to fuck me. And that's what I got. But now I want to take charge."

Maureen drew in a shaky breath and raised an eyebrow. "Well, I certainly support that plan. What do you have in mind?"

Whitney turned around completely, aware her pants and underwear were still around her calves. Somehow she didn't feel ridiculous despite that. She took the hand Maureen had used on her and lifted it, guiding it to Maureen's mouth. Maureen smiled as she took the fingers into her mouth and held eye contact as she sucked them. She let them fell from her mouth with a pop and smiled.

"Do whatever you want," Maureen said.

Whitney bit her bottom lip and arched an eyebrow.

Half an hour later, in her bedroom, Whitney's brain finally settled down to begin processing everything that had happened to her that night. The violence that started everything was just a blur, thankfully. She didn't want Bridgeman playing anything but a cameo role in her memories of the evening. She focused on the dim light of the customer bathroom, Maureen's breath on her neck and fingers inside her. She wanted to remember rising up over Maureen in this bed, the warmth of Maureen's thighs on her hips, the way Maureen's eyes had widened when Whitney guided the tip of the strap-on to her folds and then thrust inside with a single thrust of her hips.

Maureen was still breathing hard next to her. The room stank of sweat, but it was a great smell. Whitney was still wearing the harness, but it had been loosened so it wouldn't bite into her hips and leave a mark. Her left hand was curled between her breasts, which were still tender from repeated attacks by Maureen's lips and tongue. She stretched out her fingers and teased the nipple of one, hissing, then smiling when she remembered why it was so sensitive. Her right arm was underneath Maureen's shoulders, but neither of them seemed eager to free it.

"Wow," Maureen said.

"Oh good," Whitney said. "I would be embarrassed if I was the only one at 'wow.'"

Maureen rolled closer and propped herself up on an elbow. "Definitely not." She bent down and kissed Whitney. It was their softest kiss yet, and Whitney closed her eyes to fully enjoy it. When it ended, Maureen settled on top of Whitney, using her shoulder as a pillow.

"I'm going to let you decide what happens next. And don't say anything now. There's adrenaline at play, there's hormones and all sorts of extenuating circumstances. I don't regret what we did, and I don't think you do, either. I don't want you to make decisions about what it meant until you've had some time to think about it."

Whitney wanted to argue, but she had to admit there was some logic to what she was saying. She used the arm that had been pinned to pull Maureen closer and stroked her back.

"Okay." She kissed Maureen's hair. "But I'm fairly sure that this was very nice. And exactly what I needed. I know that much is written in stone."

Maureen kissed her chest. "I think we can agree on that."

Whitney closed her eyes and focused on Maureen's breathing. It prevented her from thinking about anything else that might have happened that night, or might still be happening out there in the neighborhood. Right now all she needed to do was try and stay awake until Maureen fell asleep. She had a feeling she would be able to pull it off.

CHAPTER NINE

OVER THE course of the day, Catriona confirmed that Krikor Ohanian was a big fish in a tiny pond. He was able to rule through fear because he was the biggest threat these people had ever dealt with. She quickly determined, just from following his troops and looking up articles online, that he wasn't even the scariest person in Seattle. It was a little ridiculous how much power he'd been allowed to accumulate. He didn't deserve an entire neighborhood.

Her original plan was to follow Bridgeman on his rounds, make sure he didn't set any more fires, and rob him at the end of the night. He didn't even have any backup this time, so she hadn't foreseen any problems with taking him out again.

She didn't know what had happened in the Whipjack, but she knew Reena wasn't hotheaded or impulsive enough to attack him without provocation. It ruined her plan but she could improvise.

Catriona glanced in the rearview mirror. Bridgeman was still painted in the corner of the backseat, hands resting in his lap, head turned toward the window. Something was broken in his nose; she could hear the whistle on every exhale even above the engine of her stolen car. Every now and then he made a pathetic whimpering noise and rolled his head from side to side. She'd patted him down before driving away to take away any of his weapons, but she doubted he had the ability to attack even if she'd given him a shotgun.

She parked in front of Ohanian's headquarters. The lobby was half-lit, and the security desk was vacant. It wasn't luck; she'd passed through the lobby that afternoon and seen the computers weren't hooked up and there were no phones. Ohanian was either too cheap to pay for security or he believed he was untouchable. Odds were the answer was a little of both.

Bridgeman flinched when Catriona opened the back door and climbed onto the seat next to him. He didn't move his head but turned his eyes to watch her.

"You're the one who attacked us on the bridge, aren't you?"

Catriona reached up and pressed her hand over his mouth. Her fingers on one cheek and the heel of her hand on the other, she squeezed tight enough to keep his jaw from moving. Bridgeman twisted and kicked at her, but she shifted her weight and planted a knee on his legs, pinning them down as she pinched his broken nose with her other hand. Her palm muffled his wail of pain as she squeezed the broken bone, and she felt blood pouring, but she didn't loosen her grip.

People think it's hard to kill someone. Catriona always thought it was far too easy. A slip on the stairs, a head injury, looking the wrong way when crossing the street.

Cutting off someone's air for a few minutes did the trick nicely. The fact humans only had two ways to draw in air, and both were a hand-span away from each other, seemed like the most egregious of design flaws in a body full of them. All she had to do was keep a solid grip and avoid his thrashing and it would be done.

His eyes, sunken black pits now, stared at her in terror as he struggled for breath. She returned his stare impassively. Some people tried to just stop fighting, make it look like they surrendered. Catriona knew the eyes couldn't lie. So she stared, and she saw the moment Peter Bridgeman succumbed.

She let go of his face and moved to the other side of the seat. She wiped his blood from her hands, glad she'd taken the time to put on gloves. With a quick glance out the window to make sure the street was still empty, she opened the door and hauled the dead man from the car.

His feet slid across the sidewalk as she dragged him to the door. He was a heavy fucker, but she was glad she wasn't struggling too much with him. Her strength was coming back. She felt more alive than she had in months, and she was getting stronger with every step through Ohanian's lobby.

There were several options for where to leave him. Her favorite required dragging him up two flights of stairs to Ohanian's office on the third floor. She stopped, considered whether she had that kind of energy left, and decided she did. So up she went, dragging Bridgeman behind her by the collar of his jacket. She let his feet drag; he was beyond caring so she didn't feel like she needed to take any extreme measures for his comfort.

The third floor doors had locks, but she only had to use both hands on one of them: Ohanian's actual office. Pathetic, really. She'd broken into warehouses with more complicated security measures. Hopefully the gift she was leaving would inspire them to bulk things up.

Catriona placed Bridgeman in Ohanian's chair and turned it so he was facing the door. She considered the tableau she'd created, trying to determine if it needed an extra touch. The desktop was immaculate; papers lined up perfectly square with the edges, ninety-degree angles everywhere. There were no marks or scuffs in the wood that she could see. It was a magnificent item, and she didn't feel right marring it by putting Bridgeman's feet up on the edge. It was too petty and too low reward. She decided simpler was better and tapped his head so it lolled to one side, chin on his shoulder.

With that done, she took a quick tour of the office. She didn't turn on any lights, didn't want to risk anyone spotting it and coming to investigate. But the streetlight coming in through the window helped her see what she needed to see. She examined the bookshelf, sweeping her finger along a fine layer of dust in front of the spines. She crouched in front of the visitor chair and examined the lip of Ohanian's desk. When she was done, she checked to make sure everything was as she'd found it. Then she locked the door behind her as she left the office. She stopped at the secretary's desk and did a quick inventory of everything she found there. When she was satisfied she could recite the desktop's contents by memory, she left.

She kept her eyes on the floor as she retraced her steps. Bridgeman had leaked some blood in a few places - droplets on the stairs, smears in the lobby - but they likely wouldn't be noticed before Bridgeman's body was discovered. And if they were, it didn't matter enough for her to take the time to clean it up. Ohanian would get the message regardless.

She drove back to Whipjack and found the front door still locked, and the bar was seemingly abandoned. She had a key that let her into the side stairs and she went up. She let herself into Whitney's apartment, expecting to find them both in the kitchen with a stiff drink.

Instead, the first thing she heard when she opened the door was a sharp cry. She paused and looked toward the bedroom door, which was standing ajar. She craned her neck to look inside.

Whitney was on top of Maureen, thrusting her hips forward with a strong and frankly admirable rhythm. Her arms were flexed, showing off impressive biceps currently shining with sweat. Maureen had one hand on Whitney's shoulder, the other in the small of her back, and seemed to be *guiding her movements.*

Maureen glanced toward the door and saw Catriona. Catriona touched two fingers to her brow, threw a salute, and quickly backed away out of sight. She closed the apartment door behind her as quietly as possible and headed downstairs to wait in the bar.

***

Maureen lifted her head carefully, making sure Whitney was actually asleep before she tried extricating herself. She slipped out from under Whitney's arm, sliding toward the edge of the mattress without taking her eyes off the other woman's face for signs of waking. When she was out of bed, Whitney shifted and pulled her arm against herself, curling the hand up between her breasts as she repositioned herself under the blanket.

When she fell still again, Maureen found a T-shirt on the floor near the hamper and pulled it on. Her underwear was near the door where Whitney had dropped it and she stepped into them before she left the apartment, padding barefoot downstairs to the Whipjack.

Catriona was in the bar's customer bathroom running water at the sink. She glanced up at Maureen's arrival but didn't stop scrubbing the porcelain.

"There was a lot of blood. No one should connect Bridgeman to this place, or at least not with enough evidence to get a warrant, but it's better to cover our bases."

"Sure," Maureen said, leaning against the door.

Catriona nodded toward the stairs. "Has that been going on this whole time?"

"No." She tucked her hair behind one ear, feeling like a kid caught by her mother. "Tonight was the first time."

"That's a relief. I'd hate to think I missed something that big." She turned off the tap and shook her hands dry. "How is she?"

Maureen said, "I'm not answering that."

Catriona looked at her. "*How is she*," she repeated with emphasis.

"Oh." Maureen's cheeks flushed. "Oh she, um, she's fine. Shaken up, obviously."

"It looks like you took her mind off of it."

"That was her idea," Maureen said. "Of course I didn't fight her on it."

Catriona brushed past her and went to the bar. "I'm not judging. Grab what you can when it's available, that's what I always say. She's hot. And you seemed to be enjoying yourself." She went behind the bar and crouched down to examine the contents of the cooler.

Maureen sat on a stool across from her. "I'm not talking about that with you. But I will talk about the fact you look a lot better. How do you feel?"

"Sore," Catriona admitted, popping the top of the bottle she'd chosen. "Probably a hell of a lot worse tomorrow. After this I'm going to take some painkillers and sleep until I wake up."

"If you're drinking that, you can't have painkillers."

Catriona flipped her off and took another drink.

Maureen sighed. "What about Bridgeman?"

"Dead."

Maureen stiffened. "What?"

"You didn't do it. Both of his wrists were broken. That's a hell of a way to leave someone. He would have recovered from what you did. It would've been a really shitty couple of months, but it was survivable. But I figured he was more useful as a message to Ohanian. We were probably going to eliminate him eventually anyway."

"I guess you're right. You left him at Ohanian's building?"

"In his office. His chair, actually."

Maureen whistled softly. "That's a message, all right. Do you think he'll take it?"

Catriona shrugged. "Hard to say. I guess we'll see if another building catches fire in the next few days." She raised a finger toward the ceiling. "Is that going to get in the way of your other project?"

"Why would it?"

"You might allow it to take precedence. You might have hit a wall or~"

"I haven't hit a wall," Maureen said sharply. "They're well-hidden. You know that. It's taking as long as it needs to take. And you know if you had anyone else looking, it would take *years*. It's not like you could do anything even if I had all the information available right now. You may be riding high on adrenaline now, but we'll see how you feel tomorrow morning."

Catriona grimace and finished her beer. She went to the end of the bar to put the bottle in the trash. "I'm going upstairs. Try to keep it down if you and the landlady decide to go for another round when she wakes up."

Maureen sighed and dropped her head. She and Catriona had never exactly been shy about their hookups. She'd once heard Catriona have a threesome over a live radio feed, unable to click away because there was a chance she would give a mission-vital signal and Maureen would have to act. But it had been so long since Maureen was on the other side that she'd forgotten how exposed it made her feel.

She slipped off the stool and double-checked the floor for anything Catriona had missed. She'd done a good job; the whole bar looked completely normal.

Before she followed Catriona upstairs, Maureen went behind the bar. She retrieved the discarded bottle from the trash and moved it to the recycling bin. She didn't know why she bothered other than she'd noticed Whitney took great care to separate the two, and it felt wrong to leave the error unaddressed.

With the bottle taken care of, Maureen went back upstairs and let herself into Whitney's apartment. She stripped out of her clothes and tried to crawl back into bed without being caught.

"Where'd you go?" Whitney murmured.

"Bathroom," Maureen said, kissing Whitney's chin. "Go back to sleep."

"You weren't in the bathroom."

Maureen closed her eyes. "No. But it's not important where I was. We can talk tomorrow."

"Okay. Don't lie to me, please."

"I'll do better."

Whitney put an arm around her and kissed her cheek, then her lips. "Okay. Thank you."

Maureen smiled. "You're welcome."

Whitney sighed, slipping effortlessly back into sleep. Maureen settled against her and didn't even try to sleep. She knew it would be pointless, so instead she let Whitney's breathing lull her into a meditative state and looked at the window to watch it change colors as the sun rose.

CHAPTER TEN

WHITNEY WOKE alone, but the smell of coffee told her where Maureen had gone. She sat up and put her feet on the floor. She was still naked, sore in odd places, but a quick mental inventory revealed she was happy with the way the night before had gone. She wouldn't have chosen violence against Bridgeman, but she wasn't going to regret that it happened. She hadn't foreseen having sex with Maureen, beyond passing awareness that the woman was attractive, but she was also glad that had happened. She hoped it would happen again.

She slipped on a pair of underwear and a T-shirt before she went out into the main room. Maureen was indeed in the kitchen, dressed in her shirt from the night before and a pair of shorts, her mass of hair significantly reduced by the fact it was still wet from her shower. She looked up and smiled when she saw Whitney.

"Hey. Morning."

"Hi," Whitney said.

Maureen was standing with one bare foot on top of the other, which made her look vaguely crane-like. She was pouring a cup of coffee and she pushed it across the counter toward Whitney.

"How'd you sleep?" she asked as she poured a second for herself.

Whitney said, "Very well. Extremely well." She rested her

elbows on the counter. "I don't regret it happened."

Maureen said, "Well, that's good. If you did, you might kick me out, and I can't go back to sleeping in my car after experiencing the splendor of your couch."

Whitney laughed. "I don't think you'll be going back to the car any time soon. Or the couch, either. I would like to know what it's like to wake up next to you, though."

"Sorry," Maureen chuckled. "I've never slept much and I'm used to east coast time. I wake up crazy early no matter how much I want to sleep in."

"I'll just have to keep you up later and do more to tire you out."

Maureen raised an eyebrow. "You have more?"

"Oh, I've got a vast surplus."

"I can't wait to see what you've got."

Whitney ducked her head and chuckled, embarrassed by the flush in her cheeks. How long had it been since she flirted? And with someone she'd been to bed with, and would very likely go to bed with again. Far too long.

"You should probably know that Catriona saw us."

Whitney's smile faded. "What? When?"

"Last night. While you were..." She tucked her bottom lip into her mouth and hunched her shoulders. "When you were using the strap-on, she came into the apartment. The bedroom door was open and she looked in."

The apartment felt ten degrees colder. Whitney looked around as if she expected to find someone lurking. "I didn't... She told you?"

"I saw her. I almost said something but I thought it would make you stop. And at that point, you stopping was probably the worst thing I could imagine. I'm sorry."

Whitney put her hands in her hair and scratched her scalp. She furrowed her brow as she tried to process the new information.

"No. It's okay. I-I think it would have just ruined what was a very special night. But I'm glad you told me. I guess that means she took care of Bridgeman."

Maureen's eyes widened briefly and she looked away.

"What?"

"Are you sure you don't want to take a shower before we get into everything?"

Whitney straightened. "No, I think I'm going to be using my

shower time to process a lot of things. Might as well add another to the list. What happened?"

"Last night after you went to sleep, I went down and talked with Catriona about what happened. Bridgeman is dead. She finished him off after she took him away from here."

"God." She closed her eyes. "What did she do with… him?"

"She left him in Ohanian's office."

"That's a pretty bold statement."

Maureen nodded. "She's confident there aren't any threads connecting what happened to you or the Whipjack. She's hoping Ohanian will take it to mean South Park isn't worth his time. In one month, he's had four of his guys taken out of commission either permanently or for a good long time. Eventually he's going to stop throwing more people at the problem and just seek his payday somewhere else."

Whitney said, "Or he'll try to take out his losses on us. Eye for an eye."

"That's a possibility, too," Maureen admitted. She looked up from her coffee and focused on something over Whitney's shoulder.

"What happens when you and Catriona leave? What if the people chasing you show up in a week, and next month Ohanian sends someone worse to collect the money from us? What happens then?"

Maureen pursed her lips and looked into her coffee.

"I won't leave you in the lurch."

Whitney jerked at the voice from behind her. She spun around and saw Catriona had come into the apartment without making a sound, currently standing in the open doorway.

"Jesus! Don't do that! Knock!" Whitney leaned against the counter. "How long have you been standing there?"

"She just got here," Maureen said. "I was about to say something when you asked your very valid question." She looked at Catriona. "We can't make that promise. I don't want to cut and run, but if bad people show up… I'm sorry, Whitney, but…"

"No, I understand. She can't put her life on the line."

"Of course I can." Catriona came into the room and closed the door behind her. She pointed at Whitney. "She was prepared to continue with the status quo. I'm the one who stirred up trouble. You're the one who attacked Bridgeman and forced my hand with him. We can't leave her to clean up the mess herself."

"We might not have a choice if certain people find out where you are."

"If that happens, I'll deal with it."

Maureen threw up her hands in surrender and turned away.

Whitney looked between them. "Hey, I don't want to put anyone in danger. This Ohanian guy has no idea who I am. He's never set foot in the Whipjack. There's no reason he'd come after me."

"So you're okay with him coming after one of your neighbors?" Maureen asked. "Burning down another restaurant or the tire store? Hell, he might target you completely randomly if all he wants is revenge on South Park."

Catriona said, "I'm going to make sure that doesn't happen." She checked her watch. "What time do you figure someone like Ohanian gets to the office in the morning?"

Maureen said, "He has business contacts on the east coast. He's most likely at his desk by six."

"That should be long enough, then." Catriona turned. "I'll be back."

Whitney said, "Wait, are you really going to go surveil the building right after you left a dead body in his office? He's going to have all his security on high alert. They're going to see you."

"She's not going to be hiding," Maureen said, sounding annoyed. "She's going to walk up and knock on his door."

"What?! Why?"

"Because otherwise we wouldn't be able to have a conversation on my terms. Hopefully I'll be back by lunch."

With that, she was out of the apartment.

Whitney stared at the closed door, then turned to look at Maureen. "Is she insane?"

"I think so," Maureen said, looking more annoyed than worried. "But it seems to have kept her alive this long."

The security desk was still empty when Catriona crossed the lobby. The smears of blood she'd left behind on the floor had been cleaned up, however. She took the elevator to the third floor and went directly to Ohanian's office. His secretary looked up when she appeared in the doorway, eyebrows arched and lips parting to send her away. She was mid-forties, with her graying hair done up in a severe ponytail. The nameplate on her desk identified her as Emily. Catriona spoke before the woman could get a word out.

"What the hell are you still doing up here?"

Emily blinked. "I'm~"

"He wanted you downstairs manning the front desk a half hour ago. What the hell is taking you so long? I just strolled in here."

The secretary rose from her chair, half-turning toward the office door. "Mr. Ohanian is dealing with a very sensitive matter right n~"

"No shit, Emily. Why do you think *I'm* here? Why do you think he wanted *you* downstairs at the security desk making sure the building was secure? Get down there now and pray no one slipped in any more surprises while you were up here wasting time."

She saw the conflict in the other woman's eyes, but she made the right call and hurried out the door. Catriona stepped around the desk and sat down in the still-warm chair, turning to face the computer. She tapped a key to dismiss the screensaver and scanned the desktop. She pursed her lips, shrugged, and looked for a thumb drive in the desk drawers. She saved copies of everything, unsure what might come in handy later, and slipped it into her pocket. Maureen could figure out what to do with it.

She searched the rest of Emily's desk and quickly decided there was nothing of value on it. She reached for the intercom and buzzed the main office.

"I told you not to disturb me," Ohanian snapped.

"There's someone out here who really needs to speak with you, Mr. Ohanian."

There was no response from the box. A few seconds later, the office door swung open and he stepped out, glaring down at her. Catriona turned the chair and leaned back to look at him. He was massive. Over six and a half feet, easily. Gray hair. Black shirt, black waistcoat, black blazer. His tie pin was the only flash of color; a bright dart of gold catching the overhead light. He glared at her through black-rimmed glasses.

"Who the *hell* are you?"

"I'm the delivery person who left you a package this morning. I wanted to be sure you received it safely."

He scanned the waiting room, working his jaw. "Where's Lisa?"

"Who?"

"The girl, the girl who was~"

Catriona was briefly confused. The nameplate on the desk... She realized he was the one who didn't know his own secretary's name. "Her name is Emily."

"Where is whoever was here," he snapped.

Catriona pushed herself up out of the chair, even though Ohanian was standing so close that she was almost pressed against his stomach. She tilted her head back to look up at him.

"Do you really give a shit where your secretary is, or do you want to find out why Peter Bridgeman's corpse was waiting for you when you got to work this morning?"

He glared down at her, then took a step back and swept his hand toward the office door. Catriona walked in and a man immediately approached her. She stuck her arms out to either side and patiently waited while he patted her down for weapons. He was a bit more thorough than he had to be, and she stared at his face long enough to remember him later, just in case the opportunity arose.

"She's clean," he finally confirmed.

Ohanian had reached his desk by that point. "Stupid coming here without a weapon."

Catriona walked to the guest chair and sat down. "I know what I'm doing."

Ohanian remained standing. "I assume you're the same person who has been humiliating my boys lately. You started out by handing their asses to them on a bridge, if I remember correctly."

"Yeah, that sounds like me."

He squinted at her. "You look like someone did a number on you, too."

"I've had a rough year. Who hasn't."

He crossed his arms over his chest. The sunlight coming through the window behind him shadowed his features, making him look like an ancient monolith.

"So tell me why you left a dead man in my chair this morning."

"It was a message. Leave the people of South Park alone."

He grinned. It was a death's-head mask on him. "Ah, so you're the white hat, riding in to scare off the evil rustler."

Catriona laughed out loud. "No. I'm not a 'save the day' type. But the people of South Park are good. They care about each other. And they don't deserve your men harassing them for, what, pocket money? You can't possibly be making enough money with this pathetic scam to make it worth your time. So I don't give a shit what else you do. You're obviously doing well." She gestured at the office around them. "But South Park is off limits."

"Says who?" Ohanian asked. "You?"

"Says me."

He exhaled sharply and dropped his head, considering. "Well, I may not know much about you. But I do know two things. One, you're unarmed. And secondly..."

She felt the barrel of his security guard's gun press against her hair.

"You have a gun on the back of your head."

Catriona smiled, then laughed. "Okay."

Ohanian raised an eyebrow and leaned forward, resting his fists on the desk. "I believe you should take this seriously."

"I am, Koko, trust me. I didn't just drop off a corpse and leave. I spent a little time in your office last night, so I know two things about *you*. Your desk is immaculate and there's dust on your bookshelf."

He furrowed his brow. "What does that mean?"

"Well, the first one means the guy holding this gun would never risk blowing my brains all over your desk, so there's really very little chance of him pulling the trigger."

She ducked to one side and brought her hand up in one motion, grabbing the gun from his hand with very little resistance. She used the movement to roll off the chair and landed on one knee, reaching under the chair with her free hand to retrieve the gun she'd left taped to its underside the night before. By the time she stood - one gun aimed at Ohanian and the other at his goon - they'd only had time to straighten up and stare at her with shock. Catriona used her thumb to take the safety off the gun she'd taken from the goon.

"And the dust meant you don't bother with a regular security sweep of the office, so I felt confident you wouldn't have found the weapon I left behind."

Ohanian stared at her, his mouth slightly agape. She casually looked at the gun she'd taken from the security guard.

"Oh, and your man was also technically aiming at *you*, Mr. Ohanian, considering my skull wouldn't have stopped a bullet of this caliber. A better threat would've been putting it against my temple. But I guess you don't hire these guys for their brain size, huh?"

"So you're going to kill us both?" Ohanian said.

The goon was clearly building up his courage to rush her. He was a good six inches taller than her, maybe a hundred pounds heavier, and there was a good chance even having a gun wouldn't make much of a difference if he moved quickly enough around the chair.

"Like I said, I don't give a shit about you or your business. All I want is for the people of South Park to be left alone. You do that, we won't have any further problems."

"All I have to do is get rid of you and everything continues the way it has been. Honestly I don't see much reason not to go that route."

Catriona shot the goon in the leg. When it collapsed under him, he slapped one hand down on the floor. Catriona shot it as well, relieving him of a few fingers. Ohanian jumped back from the desk and his eyes widened.

"How many of these guys do you have? Bridgeman's pals might be recovering, but this guy isn't going to be much use to you anymore with his hand like that. How many of them are you prepared to lose?"

"Only one of them has to get through your defenses," he growled.

"So far I've seen five of them, including the guy you selected to guard you on the day you found a corpse in your office chair. So I'm not exactly intimidated by anyone else you might have on your roster." She stepped around the fallen goon, keeping the guns on him as she moved toward the door. "I want you to do a thorough accounting of how much South Park is worth to you, Mr. Ohanian, and decide how many of your men it's worth to keep it. Have a nice day."

She closed the office door behind her and, as soon as she was out of sight, she started running. She tucked the guns into her belt and went for the stairs; she didn't want to get trapped on the elevator or risk the doors opening on a fully armed team when she hit the lobby. She had no idea how much security Ohanian had in the building, but she didn't want to risk more than one or two.

Fortunately the lobby was still mostly vacant when she reached it. The secretary, Emily, was standing at the security desk looking utterly lost. She turned at the sound of Catriona's running footsteps and her eyes widened.

Catriona slowed. "He's going to be pretty pissed off you just walked away and let me in. If I were you, I'd probably go ahead and quit. Right now. By following me out of here."

Emily looked toward the elevators, looked at Catriona, and then started running.

When they reached the street, Emily ran north and Catriona

headed west. She didn't wait to see if Ohanian sent out wolves. She didn't need to know what his response would be. Her only goal now was to get as far away from his building as possible so there was zero chance he could follow her to the Whipjack. She didn't want Ohanian to get the idea that attacking it, or Whitney, would be any kind of retaliation. She only wanted his rage to have one target.

Her.

CHAPTER ELEVEN

AFTER CATRIONA left, Whitney and Maureen stood awkwardly in the kitchen and waited for the other to speak first. Whitney pushed her hair out of her face and settled on one of the stools. Maureen examined the remnants of her breakfast preparation and began moving utensils to the sink.

"We should make the rounds of the other people on Bridgeman's route," Whitney said. "We can let them know he won't be coming by anymore."

"That's the absolute *last* think we're going to do," Maureen said.

"They deserve to know. Otherwise they'll be living in fear."

Maureen said, "And when word gets back to Ohanian that you're the one telling them he's gone? It's not going to take long for someone to talk. Keeping quiet is the best way to keep them safe. If Ohanian snoops around, they're going to act like people who believe he's still alive. He won't suspect them."

"I guess that makes sense."

"And it makes sense that you want to tell them the threat is gone. But honestly, we can't be sure it is until Catriona gets back from talking to him. Even then, it will be a question of how badly Ohanian wants to keep his hands on this place."

"Okay," Whitney said. "Subject change. How scared should I

be of the people looking for you?"

"Not at all. Because I'll know if they get close enough to find us. And we'll be long gone before they narrow our location down to this building."

Whitney looked at her hands. "What if I'm more worried about the part where you leave? Not because of what happened last night. Although that's part of it, I won't lie. I've gotten used to having you here. I like having a roommate. I like looking up from work and seeing you in that back booth."

"If I stay... if *we* stay, these people will eventually find us. And they'll kill us. They'll probably kill you, too, just for harboring us."

"You said this is *our* government, right? They wouldn't just..." She closed her eyes and shook her head. "Never mind. I don't know why I said that."

Maureen chuckled. "Yeah, there's always dark doings people don't like to think about. Catriona was responsible for a lot of it, actually."

"And that's why they're coming after her. And you, because you're actually the database they're so desperate to get their hands on."

"Right." She took the milk from the fridge and added it to her coffee. "So maybe they'd keep me alive. Maybe they'd keep you alive, too. Torture you in front of me as incentive to give up what I know." She took a long drink of her coffee, looking down instead of meeting Whitney's eye. When she put the cup down, she softly added, "I'd rather run and never see you again than let that happen. I've gotten used to your company, too."

Whitney's shoulders tensed. She rubbed her palms together. "Last night wasn't just about adrenaline and the heat of the moment, was it?"

"Not for me. It's fine if it was for you. I'm not going to push anything on you or..."

"It was special for me, too," Whitney said.

Maureen wet her lips and nodded. "Well. Okay, then. I guess it's good we got that out."

"Yeah."

Whitney looked out the window. "What are the odds Ohanian kills her as soon as she walks into his office?"

"I don't know what she has planned," Maureen admitted, "but I know that she's faced down people who would make Ohanian piss his pants. I'm not saying it's impossible he takes her out. Anyone can be killed crossing the street, it's all just dumb luck. But I honestly don't see Catriona being killed by someone like Krikor Ohanian."

"I guess that's comforting. In a not-comforting-at-all kind of way. It's a little scary knowing someone like her is living next door to me."

"If it makes you feel better, she's definitely decided you're one of the good ones. Once she sets her mind on someone, she rarely changes it. Plus the fact that she knows we're sleeping together now. She wouldn't turn against you and risk having me choose you over her."

Whitney raised an eyebrow. "Would you?"

"I don't know. But more importantly, she doesn't know. So I don't think she'd take the risk."

"I'll be honest," Whitney said, "it feels kind of nice to be that close to fifty-fifty."

Maureen chuckled. "Maybe sixty-forty. To your benefit."

"Good to know." She reached across the counter to get the coffee pot to pour her own cup. "I'll see what I can do to get my numbers up."

Maureen raised an eyebrow and pursed her lips.

Whitney cleared her throat. She wasn't exactly used to flirting and, even though she'd started it, she wasn't sure how to proceed. So instead, she changed the subject.

"So do you really think she can just walk into Ohanian's office and convince him to leave us alone?"

Maureen shrugged. "Sure. Ohanian is the lackey of a foot soldier of the guys Catriona is used to dealing with. She's sat down with truly horrific people before. One guy casually mentioned he had a special acid that he was going to drop in her eyes if she lied to him. She then spent the next hour lying her ass off, and got him to give up twice as much as he originally offered."

"Holy shit."

"She also knows which of her fingers would be the best to lose."

"There's a good one?" Whitney held out her left hand, spreading the fingers out. "It's the pinky, right?"

"Hell no." Maureen held her hand out as well, touching the tips to Whitney's. "The pinky is as important as the thumb. They're the bookends. They're essential for balance and properly grasping things. You lose the pinky or the thumb, you have a ledge on one side of your hand, everything gets awkward. No, you want to lose the forefinger." She tapped Whitney's with hers.

Whitney raised her eyebrows. "That's the most important one."

"It's not. If you lose it, the middle finger automatically compensates for the loss. It takes a lot less time for you to get used to its absence because it's flanked by other fingers. And the thumb, which is the actual most important one."

Whitney wiggled her fingers, trying to keep the index finger still. "Huh. I guess that kind of makes sense. How often does that come up?"

Maureen said, "Rarely, if I'm honest. The sort of person threatening to cut off one of your fingers isn't usually nice enough to let you choose."

"Not the most considerate of people."

"No."

Whitney curled her fingers protectively against her palm. "Well, I know you're a fan of my forefinger."

"The middle one is nice, too."

Whitney blushed. It was time for another subject change. "So, um. How did a nice woman like you end up being the caretaker of someone like her?"

Something changed in Maureen's face, and she looked away.

"I'm sorry. You don't have to talk about it."

"No, it's fine. I just, um..." She straightened slightly, all hint of flirtation gone in one movement. "I just don't usually talk about her with people. And to be honest, I don't agree with how you see her. I understand it. And it's a fair assessment, given the information you have. I'm not blaming you for getting her wrong. But the first thing you need to know is that you don't know her the way I do. You don't know how vulnerable she actually is."

"You just told me she lied to someone threatening to drip acid in her eyes. And you've basically told me she's stone-cold and cruel."

"There are different kinds of vulnerability."

Whitney's voice was quiet. "I know that, too."

Maureen took a long drink of her coffee and then put the mug down on the counter. "I want you to know her like I do. Or at least as anyone who wasn't there can get."

"Okay."

"Okay," Maureen said. "I told you about my mother, taking care of her. Being approached by someone who left me a card.

When Mom died, and I saw all the bills coming due with no idea what the next day would look like, I called her. She gave me an address in Gramercy Park. When I got there, she was waiting for me on the sidewalk. I expected her to take me up to some kind of office, but the stairs led down. Into a wine cellar."

*****

Maureen followed the woman, whose name she still didn't know, down into an ever-growing darkness. The stairwell was so narrow that they couldn't have walked side-by-side. It made her feel so claustrophobic that she was honestly taken aback by the expansive size of the room where they ended up. It was dimly lit from the opposite side, and rows of wine racks stood between them and the string of bare bulbs hanging on a bare-brick wall. The woman motioned for Maureen to follow her between two of the rows to the oasis of light.

There was a computer center set up beyond the wine. Four monitors, all showing security footage of various places in Manhattan. A woman was seated in front of the command center, slumped and staring at the screens without interest. She slowly turned the chair to face them as they approached. She looked past the unnamed woman and focused on Maureen.

"I know what you're going to say," Maureen's escort said. "She's not fifteen. She's twenty-two. And given how she's spent the past few years of her life, I'd say her emotional age is closer to forty. But when it comes to her computer skills, she's twelve." She turned to Maureen. "That's not an insult. My granddaughter is twelve, and I sincerely believe that girl could build a computer if I left her alone with a soldering iron and some spare parts."

The woman in the chair, Catriona, kept staring.

"I'm not sending you out alone anymore," the escort continued. "You have a choice. Either you get a partner or you get a guardian angel."

Catriona rose and moved to stand in front of Maureen. After a brief staring contest, Catriona said, "I'm going to the Manhattan Mall. If I see a single security guard before you warn me about them, you're gone."

With that, she stepped around Maureen and disappeared into the wine racks. Maureen looked at the escort.

"What is the Manhattan Mall?"

"Just what it sounds like. A shopping center, not far from here. She'll be there in about fifteen minutes." She gestured at the computers. "I guess you're going to have a trial by fire."

Maureen shrugged out of her backpack and took a seat. She tapped the keyboard and cautiously navigated around the desktop. She grew more confident as she examined the menu and saw everything available to her.

"Wow, you've got some great stuff on here."

"Nothing but the best." The escort had moved closer, her arms crossed over her chest. "Do you know how to operate it all?"

Maureen said, "If not, I'm a quick learner. Just don't pay too close attention if I'm already well-versed in some of these dark web tools."

"I'll look the other way," the escort said, amusement in her voice.

"How am I supposed to warn her about the security even if I'm able to find them? Call her cell phone? I don't~"

The escort handed her a small black box. Inside, Maureen found an earpiece.

"Just speak and she'll be able to hear you."

"Okay..."

She fitted the small rubbery bud into her ear, wrinkling her nose at how odd it felt, then focused on the task at hand. She found The Shops on a map. They had public wi-fi, which gave her access to the building's internet, which meant she could get in the backdoor of their more secure internet. The apps really were amazing, and her fingers itched to just play with some of them to see what new roads she could find. She lifted her hands off the keyboard and cracked her knuckles.

A minute later, she heard Catriona in her earpiece. "I'm approaching the entrance on Sixth Avenue."

"East side of the building," Maureen muttered, already typing. "Fortunate, since security just got an alert about a suspicious person at the Bank of America on the opposite side of the building." She typed in the report and raised her eyes to the screen. There were several blue dots on the layout of the map, and a handful of them began moving toward the bank. "And there's our security guards."

"What's sending the signal?" the escort asked.

"I asked for the location of every device logged in to the wi-fi. The stationary ones are random people surfing on their phones or doing whatever people do with public internet. Now I just isolate the mobile ones and flag them..." The blue dots turned red. "And now I'll know where they are at all times."

"You can't guarantee that's all the guards."

"No, but I can guide her better..." Her smile fell. "Except I can't see her."

"Ask her to give her location."

Maureen shook her head and started typing. "She can't just narrate her way through the store. I'm already in the security system so I'm giving myself remote access..."

One of the monitors changed to a security camera feed. She pressed her lips together, frustrated, scanning the crowd walking in front of the store.

"I can't spot her like this. And even if I did, it would only be a glimpse before she was in front of another store."

"I'm impressed you've made it this far on the fly," her escort said.

Maureen ignored the praise. She wasn't out of the fire yet. "Catriona? Can you really hear me?"

"I can."

"Go to your right, past the escalators. Stay close to the stores." She scanned the map of red dots again. "I might have sent some guards running directly at her from the other levels."

"You're doing fine," the escort said. "You just need to get her out."

Maureen rolled her shoulders and focused. "You're going to keep going..." A red dot caught her eye. "Shit! Go into Aeropostale. Someone's drifting."

A few seconds later, she heard Catriona's voice again. "I just saw him jog past."

Maureen's spirits collapsed.

"But he didn't see me. As far as I'm concerned, you're still green. Where do I go next?"

Maureen exhaled. "Close call. It'll make me be more careful." She now knew exactly where Catriona was, where the closest exit was, and she could see the red dotted security guards swirling around the bank's location like bees around a hive. Maureen accessed their alert system again and typed an update.

"Bank Suspect Spotted on 32rd Street."

The dots moved.

"Okay, Catriona, every guard is now moving to the south side of the building. You're going to leave the store you're in and head west. You're going to see the exits to your right."

There was silence for a few minutes. Maureen kept her eyes on the guards, who were now surrounding the exits on the opposite side of the building.

"I'm out."

Maureen exhaled, relieved, and slumped back in her chair.

"Good job, new girl. What's your name?"

"I'm Maureen. Uh, Rigby."

"Welcome to the team, Reena."

"Not..." She chuckled and rubbed a finger across her eyebrow. "Thanks, Catriona." She spun her chair to look at her escort. "Is that official? Am I part of the team?"

The escort said, "If that's what you can do on the fly, I can't wait to see what you can pull off when you have time to prepare. Take the weekend *to do tie up any loose ends you might have."*

"Loose ends?"

"You'll be given housing and everything else you need. You'll report back here on Monday and we'll take you to your new apartment." She watched Maureen for subtle reactions. "That's part of the job, Miss Rigby. You'll be on call twenty-four seven. If that's not acceptable to you~"

"No." She didn't have anything tying her to her old life. "That sounds perfect. Thank you for the opportunity."

The escort smiled. "We're lucky to have you, Miss Rigby. I look forward to seeing what we can all accomplish together."

"She sounds nice. Maybe not nice. But definitely not the kind of person who would torture Catriona."

"Because she didn't," Maureen said. "Her name was Fosbroke. She was the person in charge of our team. She gave us our assignments and reported to the higher-ups about our progress. She was... what was the name of the guy in the glasses on *The X-Files?*"

"Skinner," Whitney said.

"Right. She was our Skinner. Then the new management came in and..." She swept her hand in the air like clearing a table.

Whitney said, "Why would any new management want to get rid of someone as scary and efficient as Catriona? Or as talented as you?"

Maureen raised an eyebrow.

Whitney stared back, her own brows furrowed, until she realized. "I didn't think you were serious. He really burned you because you're women?"

"We had the success rate. But he wanted the company to look a certain way, and that didn't include women in the upper echelon. It's not exactly the sort of business where you can just get demoted to a desk job. Not that Catriona would have been happy about that."

"I guess not."

Maureen looked at Whitney for a long time, then seemed to come to a decision. "I want to tell you about the project I've been working on since she moved in. I'm looking for the men who held Catriona hostage. The men who hurt her, killed her a couple of times, but they were able to bring her back. They were methodical about their torture. She was useless to them dead, but they could still make her life a living hell until she gave them what they wanted. Her memories of that time are hazy, of course, but I'm making headway."

"And when you have their names?"

"That's up to her. But I have a feeling I know what her decision is going to be."

Whitney shuddered and looked away. "If these guys are anywhere near as bad as they sound, they'll absolutely deserve it. I'm sorry you had to deal with that. I'm sorry the agency became such an awful, dangerous place."

"You should know it wasn't exactly a sisterhood when I joined. I didn't find out until much, much later, but the entire time I was doing my recruitment test with Catriona in the mall, Fosbroke had her hand on the butt of a loaded gun. If I had failed, I would have been excused from the interview with extreme prejudice."

Whitney felt suddenly cold. "She would have killed you?"

"She showed me their base of operations, temporary though it might have been. She let me see her face, along with Catriona's, she gave me a phone number that could be tracked to her, and she let me play with a computer that was full of illegal and dark web tech. I was either their newest recruit or their biggest liability."

"Wow. Okay. So they've always been brutal. It just didn't matter as much when the people in charge liked you."

"Yeah," Maureen said with no shame or embarrassment. "I told you, Whitney, we're not the heroes. We're not anti-heroes. We may have done some good things along the way, but we achieved them by doing some truly awful stuff. We made deals that no one should ever have to make. No matter how much you like us, or how helpful we might seem, you should never forget that for a large part of the world, we're the villains."

Whitney sat up straighter and squared her shoulders. "I've played by the rules my whole life. Look where it's gotten me. Maybe it's time to see what being bad can accomplish."

CHAPTER TWELVE

THE NEXT few weeks were quiet and calm, but Whitney couldn't let herself enjoy it. Every morning she woke up wondering if this would be the day Ohanian struck back. It helped that she was waking up next to Maureen on those mornings, but the worry would remain until she closed the bar and headed upstairs for the night. The sound of sirens had her running for the window to see if one of the buildings next door was on fire. Everyone through the door of Whipjack after one in the morning made her heart skip a beat.

Maureen spent most nights in the back booth with her computers, scouring the internet for the men who had tortured Catriona. She was close, and getting closer every day. Catriona, meanwhile, seemed to be almost back to full strength. Some mornings she went out for a run and didn't come back for hours.

A week after Bridgeman's death, the owner of the pawn shop down the street came into the bar right after Whitney opened. He introduced himself as Jesse and, after a quick look to make sure there weren't any customers around, leaned across the bar and asked if Whitney had paid her insurance yet.

"Not yet," she said truthfully. "It's strange. Their bag-boy is usually a lot more punctual. I guess he hasn't dropped by your place, either?"

Jesse shook his head and looked out the front window. "A couple of people did see him on the usual night, but most of the places I've asked, nothing since last month. It's weird."

"Weird but good. Like a chilly day in July. Just enjoy it." She pulled a beer from under the counter. "Here. On the house."

Jesse took the bottle and lifted it in thanks. "I thought it was bad the way he dropped by every month like clockwork. But honestly this is worse. Knowing he could show up at any time..."

Whitney glanced at Maureen, who was watching her over the open laptop. Maureen subtly shook her head 'no.'

"You're already paying him cash. Don't give him your peace of mind, too. Just put the cash aside so it'll be ready when he shows up and put him out of your mind otherwise. That's what I'm doing."

Jesse sighed. "You're right." He took a drink of his beer and knocked the knuckles of his other hand on the bar. "I'll let you know if we hear anything."

Whitney nodded. "Same."

Jesse left.

"You can't tell any of them," Maureen said when they were alone again.

"I know," Whitney said. "I just can't help putting myself in their shoes."

Maureen smiled. "That's because you're a kind and sweet person. Just remember that telling them puts them at risk. They need plausible deniability."

Whitney came around the bar and sat across from Maureen in the booth. "Doesn't make it easier. Take my mind off it. How's your assignment going?"

"I'm making progress." She chewed on her bottom lip and then settled back against the vinyl of the seat. "I have two names."

"That's great... right?"

Maureen glanced toward the stairs. "I'm not sure. On the face of it? Sure, it's great news. It means we're one step closer to making those guys pay for what they did. But on the other hand, I really don't know if Catriona is up for confronting them. And what about the other three? What if I give Catriona these names, she goes after them while at half-strength, and the rest pounce on her? I could just be giving her the chance to paint a target on her back."

"So don't give her the names until you know who everyone is and where they are. Let her make an informed decision about how to attack."

"You've dealt with her for a few months now," Maureen said. "Does she strike you as the sit-and-wait sort of person?"

Whitney smiled and shrugged. "You have a point. But I think you're capable of withholding information for the greater good. She might be a little pissed when she discovers you were holding out, but having all five names at once should help smooth things over."

Maureen sighed and stretched her arms over her head. "There's also the chance she'll be angry I only have two names and rush me to get the others. Basically there's no option that doesn't give her a chance to be pissed off, so I should just relax."

"That's the spirit," Whitney said.

Maureen smiled. She reached around the computer and rested her hand on the table. Whitney placed hers on top of it.

"I like you," Maureen said.

"I like you, too."

"Even with all the baggage I come with?"

Whitney shrugged. "I honestly don't have enough information to be horrified by the truth of who you are. You told me that you killed people, not always bad people, but I guess I just don't have a rubric for what that means. Someone wanted them dead, so how innocent could they be?"

Maureen looked down at their hands and pressed her lips together. "We didn't always know one way or the other. We didn't get backstory or a full dossier explaining why the person needed to die. But sometimes we knew. Sometimes we knew, and we did the job anyway. Do you want to know about one of those jobs?"

Whitney tensed. "I don't know. Do I?"

"Good answer." Maureen took a deep breath. She looked past Whitney, eyes focusing on the far wall to avoid eye contact. "There's a leader, it doesn't matter where. He's a very bad man. Cruel, in love with power, the whole nine yards. He makes life miserable for hundreds of thousands of people. Someone wanted to stage a coup. He was making progress. Gaining followers. But certain people in power thought having the bad man in charge was good for us. Kept things unstable, kept everyone in line. So we were sent in to stop the coup. Catriona killed the man, scared off the movement. Bad man is still in power."

Whitney didn't know what to say. Part of her wanted to pull her hand away from Maureen's, but she also didn't want to send that message at what was clearly a vulnerable moment.

"You can justify anything. I know because I did. The coup was probably going to fail anyway. There would have been massive losses for the rebels, and the bad man would still be in charge. But doing it this way, we made their leader into a martyr. We inspired the people who might have died in a poorly-planned assault. Maybe they'll get stronger. Smarter. Try it again in a few years when they actually have a chance of success. It doesn't help me sleep any better at night."

"Did you ever kill children?"

"No," Maureen said immediately. "In all honestly, no one ever gave us that assignment. But I can't imagine Catriona accepting it if they did. Even sociopaths have a line they won't cross, I guess."

Whitney chose her next words carefully. "I know sometimes... the right thing can look terrible. I know sometimes terrible things can have good consequences, or lead to something great. I can't forgive or absolve things I don't know about, but I can accept you have darkness in your past. And I can work try my best not to let it color the person I see sitting in front of me."

"Thank you." Maureen's eyes were wet. "I've never told anyone that before. I've never really known anyone who knew what I did. Who I am. *What* I am."

"I'm proud to be the first, then," Whitney said. "I feel safe around you. I trust you, no matter what you might have done before we met."

Maureen closed her eyes and nodded once, then lowered her head. She put her other hand on top of Whitney's and brushed her knuckles, then pulled both of her hands back and sat up straighter.

"Right. So. We won't tell Catriona about the people I've found until I have all of them. She seems to be keeping pretty busy watching Ohanian."

"Is that what she's doing when she goes out all day?"

Maureen nodded. "She's staking out his main office. She had me find out where he lives, which was relatively easy. He's been a big fish too long and got complacent. So she's been in there a few times to see what he's up to. So far she hasn't seen any evidence he's making a move either way."

Whitney said, "As much as I want to believe he'll just cut his losses and leave us alone, I don't think he would be that generous. The principle of the thing, letting a little pissant neighborhood scare him off. I worry he's just looking for a way to turn us into an example."

Maureen shrugged. "Let him come. We'll show him just how

pissant this neighborhood really is."

Whitney smiled at her optimism and desperately wished she shared it.

Ohanian was an idiot. But he had great taste.

The only time he returned to his home, a gorgeous penthouse in downtown Seattle, was at the end of the day with an hour or so on either side of sleeping. He didn't have any security beyond that provided by the building, and Catriona was able to bypass those rent-a-cops without breaking a sweat. The first time she broke in, she spent an hour in his home office. His passwords were written on a Post-It attached to the side of his rolltop desk but she took the time to figure them out on her own just to maintain her self-respect. It still didn't take her long before she had access to everything. She saved everything that looked important to a flash drive which she later gave to Maureen "just in case it had anything useful."

The next time she spent most of the afternoon exploring his space. There were very few personal touches, to the point where she wondered if he had just left the penthouse untouched from the way the real estate agency had arranged it for potential buyers. A bookshelf in the bedroom revealed he enjoyed reading nonfiction, mostly about Eastern European politics and wars. She spent two more days searching but didn't turn up anything she could use against him. No childhood mementos, no photos of pets, not even any porn.

He was quite possibly the most boring man on the planet. But that wasn't to say her research was fruitless. The war books proved that he saw South Park as a conquered land. He was the ruler, and the protection money was fealty to his leadership. This wasn't the sort of man who would just wash his hands and walk away. He wasn't going to give up territory just because she had taken out his lieutenants.

He was planning something. So she made it her mission to find out exactly what that was.

She chose a night and broke into his office again. He'd heightened security, which made her proud, but it was still pathetically easy to get past the guards posted in the lobby. They remained at their posts and only did rounds once every hour, always at the forty-five minute mark. It only took her one night to lock in their schedules and find an alternate entrance. She was tempted to kill the guards just to send a message, but it would have needlessly complicated things. Besides, she thought it was funnier to leave them alive to face his anger.

Maureen had taught her enough tricks to go through the computers and find simple things like bank accounts, money transfers, spreadsheets, and anything she could use to piece together what someone might be doing with their money. It was ridiculous how casual people were with their financials on devices they assumed were private.

She traced a few transactions and saved the information to her phone. When she left Ohanian's penthouse, she went to a coffeeshop and started contacting the people who had received payments from him in the past month to confirm the money had been successfully delivered.

"And it's clear what services Mr. Ohanian expects you to perform in exchange for this payment?" she asked, and then took careful notes as they detailed the guidelines he'd given.

At the end of the week, she arrived at the Whipjack half an hour before Whitney was due to open. Maureen was sitting in the back booth, as always, and Whitney was behind the bar. They both gravitated toward her like moons caught in her orbit. When she sat at the end of the bar, Maureen immediately settled on the bar beside her. Whitney arrived a moment later, having stopped to get a beer from the cooler to place in front of Catriona.

"You look like you have enough information to tell a story," Maureen said.

"It might not be a nice story," Catriona said. "Ohanian is calling in favors. He's gathering forces. Mercenaries, guns for hire, basically anyone willing to break a few laws for the right price."

Whitney took a deep breath. "Okay. That's bad."

"I checked on dates with a few of them, and they were all scheduled to be in Seattle at the end of the month. I assume Ohanian is going to keep the same route Bridgeman had, but they're not going to be collecting money. He's also looking at a lot of real estate sites. I think he's going to be clearing out South Park. Getting rid of the troublemakers and replacing you with more docile tenants. Give them bottom-of-the-barrel prices to get them in, then taking the screws to them once they're locked in."

Whitney hung her head. "He's going to burn this whole place down. He doesn't know who is attacking him, so he's just going to get rid of all of us."

Catriona shook her head. "No. He won't."

"You said he's bringing an army," Whitney said.

"He's buying an army," Catriona corrected. "An army that can be bought is only worth the money in their pocket. Ohanian is just a man. He's stupid, lazy, and sloppy. He has one strategy, and that's to hit as hard as possible. If that doesn't work, he hits harder. It's worked so far because he hasn't tried hitting anyone strong enough to hit back."

Whitney scoffed and shook her head. "The bully solution? He's only brave until someone tries hitting back? You really think that will work outside a playground?"

"I'm not just going to hit him back," Catriona said. "I'm going to break his fist."

"I'm sorry I have such a strange sleep schedule."

Whitney and Maureen were lying in bed a few hours after closing the bar. They'd made love, and now they were catching their breath as the first colors of dawn began appearing in the bedroom window.

"It's not that strange to me," Maureen assured her. "Sometimes Catriona would be on a mission in Ireland while I was stationed in New York, so I would be waking up at midnight so I could be available during her daylight hours. There's really no normal when you're the lifeline for a global operative."

Whitney stroked her fingertip along a scar on Maureen's shoulder. "So is she like... an amoral James Bond?"

"I wouldn't say amoral. I've seen amoral people. Catriona is..." She shifted as she searched for the right words. "She feels things. But she can put it aside when she has to. Where you might be horrified, she would just be offended. That's why she's going after Ohanian. He's lazy and he's punching down. That's enough for her to want him stopped. She wouldn't care if he just turned around and started doing it to a rich neighborhood."

"To be honest, I don't know if *I'd* care if he was doing it to rich people," Whitney admitted.

"Yeah. So amoral is the wrong word to use for her. She just doesn't let it affect her one way or the other. But the James Bond part is pretty accurate."

Whitney stroked Maureen's back and stared at the ceiling. "I'm glad you came here to lay low. Not just for what she's doing for us. Although that's a nice bonus." She kissed the top of Maureen's head. "I think you haven't had a lot of places where you can let your guard down. And I'd like to think this is somewhere you feel safe."

Maureen lifted her head and moved up Whitney's body, pressing a kiss to her chin and then her lips. She hooked her leg over Whitney's hip under the blankets and repositioned herself until she was laying on top of her.

"This is the safest I've felt since I started working with Catriona. And before that, taking care of my mother..." Her hair fell down across her face, and Whitney reached up to brush it away. "I've never been able to just relax. There's always someone relying on me to take care of them. You don't need that from me. I can just be with you."

Whitney smiled. "That's all I need."

They kissed again. A thought occurred to Whitney, something she'd vaguely wondered before but never with this much clarity. She opened her mouth to finally ask, then closed it again and gave her head a subtle shake as if dismissing it.

"What?" Maureen asked.

Whitney pressed her lips together. "You told me that you did a background search to make sure I was trustworthy before you dropped a few grand on my bar and left Catriona here."

"Oh. Right." She lifted her head. "I didn't realize what we would become. But in retrospect, I do admit that was a violation of your privacy. I'm sorry."

"You don't have anything to be sorry for. It's your job. And you needed to keep Catriona safe. I'm not really upset about you doing that. I'm just a little concerned about what you might have found."

Maureen frowned. "About you...?"

"About my father."

"Oh. I told you I didn't find anything about him."

Whitney nodded. "And I believe you at the time. Then I learned what you can do with that computer of yours, and suddenly I'm not so sure."

Maureen shook her head. "No. Honestly, Whitney. I didn't find anything that could have led me to finding your father."

Whitney looked at Maureen's face, looking for any hint of deception. Finally she decided she was telling the truth and nodded.

"Okay."

"I've always known his name. He didn't know about me. My mother never told him, because I wasn't part of the plan."

Maureen said, "Plan?"

"Mom was a con artist. She spent a few years scamming people in San Francisco before she decided to go straight. One last big job to fund her retirement. She wanted to run a dive bar." She chuckled and shook her head. "Most people dream big. Ma wanted to serve drunks spending their last dime on piss-water. To each their own, I guess. She found a guy who was rich enough for her goals. Seduced him. Got the money she needed. Skipped town and never looked back. When she got here, she started the bar... then found out she was pregnant. I guess she hadn't factored raising a kid into her budget, so we were always scrounging for rent money."

"Wow. I can't believe your mother was a con artist..."

"Do you know what a Whipjack is?"

Maureen said, "No, actually. I never really thought about it."

"It's a beggar who pretended to be an out-of-luck sailor to get pity from passersby. Ma kind of did the same thing. She found guys who could 'save' her. She fed their hero complex and they went along with it until suddenly she was gone with half their bank account."

"So your father never came looking for her?"

Whitney shook her head. "Not that I know of. I don't think any of her victims ever came looking for her. Too embarrassed, maybe." She sighed. "So that's my deep, dark secret."

Maureen lifted up to kiss Whitney's lips. "Thank you for trusting me with it."

"You said you felt safe with me. I figured you deserved to know the whole truth."

"Thank you. Although I do still have one question. Why did you and your mother have different last names? I just assumed Mercer was your father."

Whitney shook her head. "Mercer is totally made up. Ma didn't want to saddle me with her name, and Mercer Island is where the richest richies live, so she thought it would be an aspirational sort of thing. Plus Mercer and Marchand were similar enough that it felt familial, so..." She shrugged.

"Hm. Whitney Marchand doesn't have the same ring to it. I think she made the right choice."

"Well, at least she made one in her life." She kissed the top of Maureen's head and lowered her voice. "I don't want to talk about this anymore. Okay?"

"Okay." Maureen shifted. "If you want me to change the subject, I was going to mention that this is the longest relationship

I've ever had with anyone. So I don't know when it's too early to say... certain things. I don't want to jump the gun, but I also don't want you to think I'm... not... thinking it. Does that make sense?"

"I love you, too," Whitney said.

Maureen smiled and raised her eyebrows. "Not too soon?"

"It's been a few weeks," Whitney chuckled. "I've said it sooner. Regretted it. Took longer, and regretted that, too. So I don't think there's a real good time table for it. Just when it feels right. And it feels right, right now."

"Yeah." Maureen put her head down on Whitney's shoulder.

Whitney smiled. "You didn't actually say it..."

"I know. But I'm thinking it. And I'll find a good time for it."

Whitney laughed and kissed the top of Maureen's head. "I'll be waiting."

Chapter Thirteen

The end of the month arrived, and Whitney found herself unable to focus on anything for more than thirty seconds at a time. She brought up the idea of everyone closing up shop for the night, just a full blackout, but Catriona rejected that plan. "Right now, we have the advantage of knowing when they're coming for you. If you close up, you force them to choose a new date, one we may not be able to guess. It's far better to make them come to us."

Knowing it was the best strategic move did nothing to calm her nerves. She jumped at every customer who came in the door, and her distraction led to a much higher ratio of drinks being poured wrong than usual.

Maureen was there for moral support, taking a break from her investigation so she could give her full attention to the current situation. She'd bought a drone online because she was so accustomed to having an "eye in the sky" for missions like this. Whitney didn't know where she'd gotten the high-tech machine that arrived, some kind of cross between a wasp and a spider, but it damn sure wasn't Amazon.

When Whitney came over to place a bottle next to Maureen's laptop, she glanced at the screen. She was currently watching a live feed from the drone's camera as it ran along the southern border of the neighborhood.

"No unusual activity to report yet," she said, then glanced up at Whitney. "How are you doing?"

"Holding it together. Barely. Catriona didn't even tell me where she was going when she left."

Maureen shook her head. "Me neither. But there are really only two options. She said Bridgeman used to start at the south edge of the neighborhood and work his way north across the bridge. There's no reason to assume this army of Ohanian's will change things up. He wants to send a message. That's the whole point of doing it tonight. So there's a chance she'll be waiting where she saw Bridgeman park, because the odds are with her."

"And if she's not there?"

"Ohanian's office. All his muscle is bound to be focused on South Park, so he'll be at his most vulnerable tonight."

Whitney said, "*We're* at our most vulnerable tonight."

Maureen nodded. "That's a fair point. Yeah. So my money is on the first option." She reached over and put her hand on top of Whitney's. "Whatever happens, you'll be safe. I promise."

"I know."

"Because I'm here. And I love you."

Whitney smiled and huffed out a laugh. "You chose well."

"Thank you."

Maureen turned her attention back to the screen. Whitney went back behind the bar, wondering how long it had been since someone had said those words to her. Quite a while, and a time span she didn't want to put a number on. She only hoped it was a sign of how the night would go, rather than the universe tossing her a bone before everything went to hell.

For now, all she could do was wait.

If Catriona hadn't been aware of the drone, she doubted she would have noticed the low hum of its engine as it buzzed overhead. She touched two fingers to her eyebrow and tossed off a salute to the machine, even though she couldn't see it and doubted Maureen could see her on the live feed. She was crouched in an alley that gave her a panoramic view of the street in front of Tide City Laundry. She'd found Bridgeman's schedule in a ledger on Ohanian's computer, and the laundromat had always been the first stop on his monthly rounds.

She'd only been waiting twenty minutes when she heard the rumble of heavy truck engines coming from the direction of the bridge. She tensed and pressed her shoulder to the brick wall. She held her breath and stayed completely still, becoming part of the environment. The first truck came around the corner, followed by a second and a third. They parked along the curb across from the laundromat and men began climbing from the trucks.

Catriona counted seven of them in total: three in the first truck, two in the others. They were dressed similar to her, all in black with tactical vests and knit caps currently pushed up to reveal their faces. The driver of the lead truck held up two fingers and pointed them at the laundromat, and two men broke off to cross the street. They both carried long aluminum bats, and one man swung his as if getting used to the weight. The rest of the men remained by the trucks.

Catriona jogged to the end of the alley, to the laundromat's dumpster. She crouched next to it and retrieved the black duffel bag she'd stashed there earlier. She'd expected to be outnumbered. The best defense for that was to be prepared, and she had the advantage of knowing where the fight would happen beforehand. Two at a time was much better odds than she'd been anticipating. She straightened, pressed a hand to her ribs to make sure there was no lingering tenderness, then carried the bag to the laundromat's back entrance.

It was unlocked, so she let herself in. The door led to a small office, where an elderly man was hunched over a desk with a hardback book open in front of him. He was staring at her, mouth open with shock and fear. Luckily he was too terrified to make a noise. She held her hand up with a finger across her lips, then she spread her fingers in the universal signal to stay calm.

"I'm here to help you. The danger is—"

A whistle came from the front of the store. "Hello-o-o... Anybody home?"

She pointed. "Out there. Will you let me help you?"

His jaw trembled and he looked to the office door, then back at her. Glass shattered in the main room, and the thugs called out another mock greeting.

The old man flinched. "A-are you... the good guy?"

"No," Catriona said. "But right now I'm all you have. Is anyone else here?"

"Just me," he said.

"Then go out the way I came. Don't go out onto the main road, but get as far away from here as you can. You got that? Side streets. Alleys. Don't go to the front of this building."

He stared at her.

"*Now,*" she hissed.

He jumped up from his chair and hurried past her to the door. Catriona put down the bag, unzipped it, and took out her supplies: googles, two retractable batons, and two squat canisters that looked like beer cans. Glass broke out in the main room of the business, and the men laughed.

"If you want to hide under your desk, we can wait!"

Catriona put on the goggles and hooked her forefingers around the pull-rings on the cans. She moved to the office door and tossed them underhand into the main room. Blue smoke began pouring out of the grenades as soon as the rings had been pulled free, and Catriona pulled her knit cap down over her face before she stepped through the smokescreen.

"The hell is this?" one of the men asked, and then immediately began coughing.

Catriona extended her batons by flicking her wrists and followed the sound of coughing. The first man she came to, a shadowy ghost in the smoke, turned toward her just as she cracked him across the jaw. He went down hard and his friend tried to rush her. She stuck her other baton straight out and he ran into it, folding in double as she dug the tip into his stomach to shove him backward. He collapsed on the floor and she turned her attention back to the first man.

He was slumped against one of the washing machines. She brought the baton down on his fingers, smashing them against the machine, and then hit him across the face again. He dropped to the ground and made no attempt to get back up. She kicked him hard in the gut and stepped over him. The other man, still bent in half with one arm across his stomach, was lurching toward the door. His cough sounded painful, like maybe there was blood coming up with it. She brought her baton down on his neck and he dropped, down for the count.

Catriona grabbed his collar and pulled him away from the door. She snagged the other guy as well, dragging them toward the back room.

"You broke my jaw, you asshole," the first guy slurred.

She propped the men up next to each other against the back wall. The smoke had mostly dissipated now, and she could see the weapons they'd brought with them.

"I made a decision to *not* make a decision," she said, half to herself. "I said I wouldn't make a decision on how far I'd go and I'd let the weapons you brought with you as guidance."

She unhooked the gun from one man's vest and checked the ammunition.

"This is not terror. This is not intimidation. This was brought for murder. So..."

She shot both men in the head, one bullet each. Then she stood and started running in the same motion, slamming her shoulder into the back door to open it. A quick scan of the alley told her no one was waiting so she didn't slow down.

The second stop after the laundromat was an all-night diner. It was only a block away, but she didn't know how long the remaining five thugs would linger before moving on. They could have already arrived. When she got to the right street, she left the alley so she could get an idea of the situation. The heavy truck they'd arrived in was rolling slowly down the street, and she ducked back into the shadows. She was still wearing her cap and the goggles, so she doubted they'd seen her, but there was no sense in tempting fate.

The truck stopped and one man hopped out. She dubbed him Three. He adjusted his shirt with one hand, the other holding something bulky against his side. He stalked across the street, head on a pivot for any potential witnesses. The diner's lights were on, illuminating the sidewalk directly in front of the business, and Three stopped in front of the windows and brought up the bulky object. Catriona could see now that it was a gas can, which he was uncapping.

She looked down at the guns she'd taken from One and Two. There was no chance they'd loaded incendiary bullets, and she hadn't thought to pack any. Besides, when she looked again, Three had already started pouring gas along the foundation of the building. If she ignited it, the fire would just spread to the building anyway.

The truck was already rolling again. Whoever was in charge probably expected each goon to take their time at each stop and then catch up further down the road.

Catriona leaned out just enough to aim one of her stolen guns. She squeezed the trigger and a bloom of blood erupted on the side of Three's head. His legs went rubber and he dropped the gas can as he fell. Catriona ran along the sidewalk and banged her hand on the front door of the diner. She didn't want these people to be unaware of the gas spill on their sidewalk.

She sidestepped Three and continued down the street, chasing the taillights of the truck as it rolled patiently toward its next target.

Three men down.

Four to go.

Emmett Baker stopped in the middle of the street. The truck hummed and rumbled around him. It was like a living creature, just one more member of his raiding party. He liked to think of himself as a Viking. A proud warrior on a mission. Their next stop was in a strip mall. He hated that term. It sounded seedy, cheap. He looked at the list he'd been given, then looked out the window to confirm the names of the businesses.

Three businesses: a vape shop. Massage parlor. Liquor store. There were three men left in the truck with him. It was a perfect alignment, and it pleased him.

"One each," he said.

"Who goes where?" one of the men asked.

"You decide."

The men got out of the truck and crossed the parking lot to the long building with its multiple storefronts. He checked his watch. They would wait here for the other three to finish their work and catch up. Then they would continue on to the next business on his list.

A bar called Whipjack.

He faced forward, one hand resting on the steering wheel, the other holding a gun on his lap. He could wait for hours like this. It was all a matter of training his mind to be still, to appreciate the silence. To be aware of—

The passenger door of the truck opened and someone climbed in. He snapped his head around, confused how any of the men could have completed their task already. That was the only reason the woman was able to reach across the console and pull the gun from his hand without any struggle. She shut the door behind him and settled in the seat like it was her car and she was reluctantly allowing him to be behind the wheel.

"I'm calling you One," she said. "If you want me to use your name, you can give it to me."

He glared at her. She shrugged.

"I found your name in Ohanian's ledgers anyway. Emmett Baker got paid the most, which I assume would make him the leader, and the leader is the guy who gets to stay in the truck while everyone else gets sweaty." He looked at her with something close to approval. "My name is Catriona Hendrix. I haven't decided yet if I'm going to kill you tonight. Although it's certainly much more likely now that I told you my name. But I figured since you were alone, we could take the opportunity to have a conversation."

"Who are you?"

"We covered that. The question is, who are you? Do you actually care about what you're doing, or is it just a paycheck?"

He faced forward. "I get hired for a job. I do the job."

"Destroy one man's business, burn down a family's diner, doesn't matter to you. As long as you get paid. I get that. Work is work. People like us, we don't get to do normal jobs. Clean jobs. Do you think you could work in a laundromat? Or a gas station?"

"No," he said.

She nodded. "Me neither. It's just not in our blood." She pressed her lips together. "So since this is just a job to you, I'm asking you to quit."

"That wouldn't do very much for my reputation."

"Ohanian won't be around to badmouth you. All these people out here? They're just trying to make a living. They help people. What's the point of ruining their lives, and making it harder for some random person to do their damn laundry? It's stupid and it annoys me. So I'm definitely killing him tonight. So everything you're doing here is pointless. You're just carrying out the wishes of someone who won't matter in a couple of hours."

"You're going to kill Ohanian?"

She nodded.

He looked at her again. She was a tiny person. He had seen too many ferocious women to discount her on the basis of gender, but she was definitely on the small side. She wouldn't be intimidating in the slightest without her weapons. He looked down at her hands, wondering how fast she was. Small people could be very deft when necessary.

The passenger door of the truck opened. The man who had started to climb in had time to register the woman in his seat and say "Hey~" before she shot him in the head. She had kept her eyes on Baker, simply swinging her arm around like it was clockwork. He fell back onto the pavement, and Catriona swung the gun back around to focus it on Baker before he could even think about moving.

"He probably came back from the vape shop because the door was barricaded. I knew where you'd be stopping tonight. I had time to get ready."

"What about the massage parlor and the liquor store? If the men I sent there are on their way back~"

"They're not," Catriona said. "They got inside. But they'll wish they didn't. The vape shop is owned by a Marine. I dropped by. Told him what he could expect tonight. He was waiting. As for the massage parlor... you'd be surprised how many cops they have on their client list. I asked the owner to give them a call. They aren't what you'd call the most honest cops on the force." She chuckled. "I mean, they're regulars at a jerk joint. So I don't think you're friend is going to be officially booked tonight. But he's not coming back."

Baker was breathing hard now. "What about~"

"The men you left behind? Dead." She nodded. "So it's down to you. I could just put a bullet in your head now and call it a night. But I'm willing to let you decide. You could finish the list on your own, I'm sure. But at this point, is it really worth your time and effort? Do you want to die for someone you know is going to lose in a few hours anyway, or do you want to call this job a wash and go home, wait for the next one? I could go either way. You're a person who hurts people for money, so I won't lose any sleep about taking you out. But I don't have any particular reason to kill you, either. So it's up to you."

Baker considered, then decided it wasn't worth the trouble. He held his hands up and nodded. "Okay. I'm not going to lose anything else on this job. You win."

"Good. Out of the truck."

"What?"

"Get out of the truck. I'm not going to kill you, but I'm not going to give you the chance to run me down with this thing." She gestured with the gun. "Start walking."

Baker rolled his eyes and opened the door. "I could use people like you. And if you're telling the truth, I've got a lot of positions just opened up. You interested?"

Catriona shook her head and pointed the gun again. "Move."

"All right. Well, you know my name, so you know how to get in touch with me."

He opened the door and stepped out.

Catriona made a noise of irritation. "Oh, damn it. I told you my name. Stupid, cocky, show off..."

Brown turned around as she brought the gun up.

"Sorry, Emmett. You understand."

He was surprised he remained conscious long enough to feel his body hit the pavement, and then nothing else.

CHAPTER FOURTEEN

WHITNEY KEPT jumping every time a car passed, so eventually Maureen ordered her to come over and join her in the booth. She put her hand under Whitney's hair and alternated between massaging her neck and playing with her earlobe. Whitney tried to stay vigilant, but it wasn't long before the steady pressure did the trick and she felt the tension seeping out of her.

"That's not fair," she muttered, pressing back against Maureen's hand. "I need to stay vigilant."

"You know if any of these bad guys got past Catriona, there's not much you and I will be able to do against them."

Whitney opened one eye, looking askance at Maureen. "That's not helpful."

"I know. I've never really had to comfort anyone before. Maybe checking in with the drone will help."

"Maybe."

Maureen used one hand to access the feed, then guided the drone back to the laundromat. It was immediately apparent something had happened. Smoke was trickling out through the open front door, and a man was pacing on the sidewalk with a phone to his ear. Whitney motioned for Maureen to continue, and she flew the drone toward the diner. A group of people were there, using a pressure washer on the sidewalk. They all had bandanas pulled up over their noses, and it looked like a dead body was lying in the gutter.

"That's a corpse, right?"

"Looks like a corpse," Maureen confirmed.

Whitney shuddered. "They're just... ignoring it?"

"Probably called the cops. You live here. Whatever they're spraying obviously reeks. Probably gasoline. Dead guy was probably trying to burn the place down and caught a bullet first."

"From Catriona?"

"That's who I'd bet on, yeah."

Whitney pressed against Maureen's side. "Go on. The next one is the, um, the liquor store, I think. And the strip mall."

"Yeah," Maureen said, moving further north.

Two dead bodies were sprawled a few feet apart in the strip mall parking lot. From above, Whitney thought it looked like the driver and passenger of a vehicle had been thrown out, and then the car was driven away.

"Do you think that's all of them?"

"No way to know. Catriona said something about Ohanian hiring seven people, and I only counted three corpses. But who knows what was inside those businesses."

Whitney swallowed the lump in her throat. "We're... we're next on the list."

"Mm-hmm," Maureen said.

They both looked at the door. Whitney listened for sounds, any hint of someone trying to break in or pour gasoline along the foundation. The building remained frustratingly silent.

"If they were already at the strip mall, then they should be here already," Maureen whispered.

"Mm-hmm. If they're coming."

Maureen nodded. "And if they're not coming, Catriona should have stopped by to give us an update. Either way... someone should be here."

Whitney said, "So where is she...?"

Maureen shook her head and, to Whitney's growing panic, actually looked worried.

Catriona had followed Ohanian's schedule close enough to know he wouldn't be in his office, but there was a chance he stayed late so Baker's team could report in. She drove past his building to confirm his office windows were dark before she continued on to his home. Part of her wanted to crash through the front door, take out the doorman and security, then storm up the stairs like some kind of one-woman army, but she didn't want to give him any extra time to prepare.

So this would be a quiet assault.

She parked Baker's truck in the alley and used the same service entrance she'd accessed multiple times in the past for her fact-finding missions. The stairwell door was locked, maybe some kind of after-hours precaution, but it only slowed her down by a few seconds.

At Ohanian's floor, she braced herself to find anything in his penthouse. He could have associates with him, perhaps a secretary or a gofer. She'd never seen any evidence of a romantic partner, but that didn't preclude the possibility of one-night stands, mistresses, escorts. She drew her gun, screwed on a silencer, and listened at his door for any sounds within. When she heard Ohanian cough, she stepped back and shot the lock off.

Ohanian was halfway to his desk when she kicked the door in. She shot the wall in front of him and he recoiled from it. He was far from the imposing figure he cut in his office, clad in silk pajamas under a white robe, hair shaggy, and cheeks stubbled with salt and pepper whiskers. He was still over a foot taller than her, so when he saw who had entered his home, he charged her.

Catriona fired again, the muffled WHUMP drowned out by his cry of pain as the bullet sliced past his calf. He dropped to one knee as if he had changed his mind and wanted to propose instead. She kept the gun steady on him as she advanced.

"Emmett Baker. John Bloom. William Boggan. James Curtis. Edward Fields. Oscar Dow. Perry Speer. I'm sure you recognize those names."

Ohanian bared his teeth. "I'm going to make you regret this, you bitch."

"I gave you a chance, Koko. I had no problem with someone running a business, even if it wasn't legitimate. But I told you to stay away from this people. And what did you do? You tried to be a big man. You tried to be a tyrant. But you're a lousy tyrant, Koko. And lousy tyrants get deposed. Violently."

He held his hands up, palm out. "What do you want? Money. I can give you money."

"I have money. You don't have anything to negotiate with,

Koko. I gave you a chance to back out, and you lobbed a grenade. I took that personally. It meant you didn't respect me enough to listen. So now you have to learn a lesson."

"Consider the lesson learned. I'll go somewhere else. There are other neighborhoods like this. I can rebuild, find more heavy lifters to do the legwork." He chuckled. "How about you? As far as auditions go, you've made a hell of an impression on me. You'd be an amazing lieutenant. A second in command."

"Sounds like a great way to buy time so you can shoot me in the head when I least expect it." She tilted her head to the side. "But you bring up a good point. After I get rid of you, I'm not sure what exactly my purpose will be. It's one of the strange things about being tortured for so long you basically decide you're just going to die and there's no way around it."

She moved to the armchair next to the coffee table and sat down, leaning forward so she could keep the gun on Ohanian.

"I actually was dead a couple of times. Fuckers revived me so they could keep torturing me. I figured eventually they would go too far and I just wouldn't wake up. And then I got out, but I was so hurt I figured it was only a matter of time before my body gave out. But I kept healing. I got better. And now, this whole little endeavor has proven I'm almost back to my old fighting weight. So it begs the question, what *do* I do now...?"

She looked toward the window as her voice trailed off, lost in thought.

Ohanian dived for the coffee table. He grabbed the gun that was concealed underneath it. Sprawled on his side on the floor, he swung it around and pulled the trigger.

It clicked on an empty chamber.

Catriona looked toward him as if he was a waiter who had dropped a tray. "I've spent more time in this penthouse the past few weeks than you have. Come on, man. I planted a gun in your office. Why wouldn't you take that as a signal to, I don't know, do a sweep of your damn home?" She sighed and stood up. "See, this is why I could never work for you, Koko. I may not have liked my former bosses, but I could at least respect them."

She took the gun from him and tossed it across the room.

"My bosses. That's one thing I have to fill some time. I know my girl has more information than she's giving me on their whereabouts. She's probably waiting until I wrap up this whole thing before she distracts me with it. That makes a lot of sense. But even that won't take too much of my time. I was an operative. I traveled the world doing missions. What am I supposed to do now? I need a purpose."

"Look," Ohanian said, true fear finally creeping into his voice. "You can't just eliminate me, all right? There will be a vacuum. Someone will come in and take over in my absence."

Catriona raised an eyebrow. "Now there's an idea. But I don't really want to become a kingpin. Seems like an awful lot of work."

"We can make a deal."

"You really only have one tool in your belt, don't you? I'm not joining forces with you. You're not surviving tonight. I'm just thinking out loud and waiting to see if your security ever shows up." She glanced at the door and then looked at her watch. "It would really be easier to bottleneck them at the door, but honestly I'm starting to think they're not coming."

"You used a silencer," Ohanian said.

Catriona said, "You still used the silent alarm as soon as I came in." She looked at him. "You *did* hit the silent alarm under the desk before... oh for God's sake, you just went for the gun?" She rolled her eyes, her irritation at the man's incompetence boiling over. "You thought you could take care of me yourself so you didn't even bother... fuck, you know what?"

She shot him in the head.

"You're not even worth the lecture," she told his corpse. "You only had one talent: money and a talent pool of tough guys too stupid to realize they were being paid by an imbecile." She kicked him over onto his back. She'd planned to make it look like a suicide, but that wasn't possible with a wound in the front of his skull. Instead she retrieved the gun she'd tossed aside and placed it in his hand. Then she emptied her clip into the wall to make it look like the kill shot had just been a lucky hit. He was sure to have enough enemies to make an assassination possible.

"Just so disappointing, Koko. Damn."

She didn't bother closing the door behind her when she left. The building had security cameras, but she'd figured out how to get past them the first time she visited. A cakewalk. The entire mission had been like learning to ride a bike with training wheels. She was sure Ohanian was impervious but a lot of standards, and he was the sort of person who seemed above the law because he could pay off any cop who came sniffing around, but she was still shocked by how easy it had ultimately been to eliminate his threat.

Downstairs, she sat behind the wheel of Baker's truck and considered her options. Ohanian was dead. All the men he'd hired were dead. She hadn't found any evidence of a higher-up pulling Ohanian's strings, so she didn't have to worry about a bigger fish coming for revenge. Ohanian was probably right about the vacuum, but how many people would really care about a run-down neighborhood on the ass-edge of Seattle?

She started the truck and pulled away from the curb. Questions about the future were the definition of bridges she could wait to cross.

There were customers throughout the night, and Whitney tried her best to act normally when she served them. She was pretty sure no one picked up on her anxiety, even though she only gave terse replies to their questions and basically ignored them in favor of staring at the door and drumming her fingers on the bar in a rapid staccato rhythm.

It was almost closing time when Catriona finally came through the door. Whitney's breath caught in her throat, and Maureen was up and out of the booth before she managed to remember how to form words.

"Where have you been?" Maureen asked.

"Taking care of things," Catriona said. "The goons Ohanian recruited had trucks I needed to take care of. Then I checked to make sure everything was okay at the first places they stopped."

Whitney said, "I guess you managed to take care of all of them? We saw... b-bodies on the drone footage."

Catriona nodded. "Ohanian, too."

Maureen raised her eyebrows. "You mean..."

"Dead. Ridiculously easy. I'm almost embarrassed." She pointed at a bottle on the shelf behind Whitney. She took it down and handed it over, too shell-shocked to speak. "I almost wish I'd left him a weapon or something. It would have been a little more sporting."

Whitney touched two fingers to her forehead. "So... wait. I'm sorry for being dense. But does this mean it's over? Ohanian is dead, and all of his guys are gone, and the guys he hired are dead..."

Catriona shrugged, swallowing the mouthful of beer she'd just taken. "I would assume so, yeah. He was preying on this neighborhood because it seemed like an easy target. Anyone coming in to take over is going to look at the body count and hopefully think twice about taking a swing at it. For now... Whitney, can I have another bottle?"

"Uh, sure." Whitney got it and handed it to her. "For now, I'm going upstairs to get some sleep. You two can do the same. Or do whatever it is you do once this place closes down." She winked and took both her bottles to the stairs. "Have a good night, ladies."

"You too." Whitney was still stunned by the idea that it was over. Ohanian. Bridgeman. The thousand-dollar payoffs. She felt a hand on top of hers and looked at Maureen. "Hi."

"Hi." Maureen smiled. "You okay?"

"I don't know." She turned her hand over and brushed her fingers over Maureen's palm. "I think I want to close early."

Maureen nodded. "Okay. And then what?"

Whitney chuckled and shook her head. "I honestly don't know."

Whitney tried to distract herself by spreading Maureen's red hair across her bare thighs like a shawl. There was so much of it when she let it loose, layers and layers, and she loved the way it felt when she ran it through her fingers. But even with the hair to distract her, Maureen was far too talented for her to hold off the inevitable for long. Soon she was breathing heavily, her fingers curling on the back of Maureen's head, and her lips pulled back against her teeth in a long, drawn-out moan of pleasure and release.

Maureen kissed Whitney's thigh, then her stomach, and wrapped her arms around Whitney's waist and stretched up to kiss her properly with wet lips.

"That seemed to take a while," Maureen murmured playfully. "I must be losing my touch."

"Not at all." Whitney stroked Maureen's cheek. "I'm sorry. I just... I-I didn't want it to end."

Maureen smiled. "Well, we can rest and do it all over again." She kissed the corner of Whitney's mouth, her hands roaming to new parts of Whitney's body. "I have some ideas for what we can do in the meantime, if you've still got the energy."

Whitney gently pulled Maureen's hands away from her, prompting the kisses to end.

"Whitney? Are you okay?"

"Yeah. But I... I don't... I..." She inhaled and finally met Maureen's eyes. "You're going to leave soon. Catriona took care of Ohanian. She's obviously well enough to move on to whatever is next for the two of you. And you always said it was safer to keep moving, right? Harder to find a moving target. So I'm trying really hard to appreciate the time we still have together, but also I think if we're going to call it quits soon anyway, it'll be easier..."

"Shh, stop." Maureen stood up and stepped forward, straddling Whitney and sitting on her lap. She put her hands on Whitney's shoulder and looked down at her. "I don't know what Catriona is going to decide, but I also don't think she's planning to leave any time soon. She's been safe here and we don't have any reason to believe that will change."

"You have most of the names she's looking for," Whitney said. "When you have them all~"

Maureen put a finger across Whitney's lips. "We'll deal with that when the time comes. For now, I'm just going to enjoy the beautiful woman I'm sitting on. And I would like you to appreciate that fact as well."

Whitney couldn't help herself from smiling. "It is pretty easy to appreciate."

"Yeah?" She started rocking her hips. "You got any ideas about what to do about it?"

As it turned out, they both had a few ideas.

CHAPTER FIFTEEN

THE WEEK after Ohanian died was the busiest South Park had seen for a long time. The police descended on the neighborhood like cicadas, a horde only seen once in a generation in response to the bodies found littering the streets. Every business owner and resident was questioned multiple times, but no one saw anything that might help with identifying the culprit. Whitney claimed to have had a very quiet night, no sign of any violence whatsoever at the Whipjack. Eventually it was discovered that the dead men were apparently all killed with their own weapons, which was enough for the police to close the cases and move on.

Alternatively, as far as Catriona could tell, there was no investigation whatsoever into what happened to Krikor Ohanian. She checked on his penthouse and office regularly but she never saw a police presence. When she decided to take the risk to actually ride the elevator up to his floor, planning to play a lost and confused cleaning woman if she was confronted, she saw that his front door had been repaired as if nothing had happened.

When she returned to the Whipjack to report the news that Ohanian seemed to have been disappeared, she found Whitney and Maureen sitting together in their usual booth. They looked like parents on the verge of announcing their divorce. Catriona sat across from them and gestured with her hands that she was ready for whatever they had to say.

Whitney looked at Maureen, who cleared her throat and took a notepad from her pocket. She placed it on the table and pushed it across to Catriona.

"That's a list of the names and current locations of the men who held you captive. The men who tortured you."

Catriona tensed. "All of them?"

"You said there were five. I found the five."

"How long have you had this?"

Maureen tapped her fingers on the table to buy herself a few seconds. "I've had some of the names for... a little while. The final name, I didn't get until last night. I didn't want to give it to you piecemeal. I thought you'd want the whole thing at once so you could—"

Catriona held up her hand to cut off the excuse. Maureen pressed her lips together.

Catriona took a breath and flipped the notebook open to the first page. Maureen had dedicated one page to each man, their name written across the top line with all the other pertinent information listed underneath. For the moment, she ignored the technical details and only read the names.

Silas Perry. Franklin Warner. Benjamin Taylor Reese. Arthur Ford. Robert Kennedy.

These were the men who had betrayed her. Held her hostage. Made her something less than human. Killed her.

Catriona curled her fingers in, made a fist, squeezed. She remembered the pain. Electrodes attached to her skin, the electricity making her brain short-circuit. The anguish when the voltage was stopped. The way it felt when one of the men - Benjamin? Silas? - had casually broken her finger like it was a dry twig. Their faces were impassive, their eyes flat as they considered which finger would cause her the most pain.

"Are you okay?" Whitney asked.

Catriona looked at the women across from her. "Did you hold this back until I dealt with Ohanian for you?"

"No!" Maureen said immediately. "That didn't factor into our thinking at all."

"I wouldn't blame you if it did," Catriona said. "It would have been a potential distraction. If I'd let my attention slip that night, one of those assholes might have gotten the drop on me. I was just curious if the timeline was as fortuitous as it seemed."

Maureen said, "It was a while ago when we made the decision about when to give you the names."

"We." Catriona looked at Whitney. "You're 'we' now. Making decisions about me together?"

Whitney started to answer, but Maureen beat her to it. "Yes."

Catriona nodded slowly, processing that information along with everything else.

Maureen touched the notebook with one finger. "Silas Perry was the first name I uncovered, and he's currently in Manhattan. There's absolutely no way for you to get there without hanging a big flashing beacon around your neck for the others to follow. I figured it was safer to know where they all were before we even discussed the plan."

Catriona inhaled and looked through the notebook again. None of the men were in Seattle, or anywhere close to the Pacific Northwest. That was lucky for her, when she was still vulnerable, but it was irritatingly unfortunate now that she was ready to go after them.

Whitney cleared her throat. "It... wouldn't be impossible for her to get to New York anonymously."

Both of the women looked at her. Catriona was surprised to see Maureen also hadn't been expecting that interjection.

"Explain," Catriona said.

Whitney pressed her lips together and shifted in the booth. She looked at Maureen and reached out to take her hand.

"My mother was a con artist. She had a different name everywhere she went. Which means she also had identification."

Maureen was already shaking her head. "I appreciate the thought, but there's a huge difference between passable IDs back then and what Catriona would require now. We could get a fake ID that could get her past security at the airport, but the people we're hiding from know what to look for. She would stick out like a sore thumb."

"It's what we used to do," Catriona said. "The majority of people I targeted didn't want to be found. They all used fake IDs that they thought were uncrackable."

"So?" Maureen said. "What are you going to do?"

"I don't know," Catriona said. "I need..." Her voice trailed off, and she shook her head. "I don't know. But I'll figure it out. Thank you, Maureen. For everything."

Maureen had been looking at the notebook, but she raised her head in surprise. "Oh. You're... welcome, Catriona."

Catriona nodded and started to slide out of the booth, then stopped.

"What is it?" Maureen asked.

"The people I was hunting didn't want to be found. But I found them anyway. And I'm ready to move mountains to get to them." She scanned the table like she was reading a book only she could see. "Anyone would react the same way if they suddenly got a bead on someone they're hunting."

Whitney straightened, realizing what she was getting at. "You can't get to Manhattan without them being ready for you. But you can bring them here. You can act like you got sloppy. Get caught using a fake ID. Send up a red flag."

Maureen held up a hand to stop their momentum. "Okay, yes, they'll probably send *someone*. But there's no way these five will come themselves."

"They already got their hands dirty once," Whitney said. "They tortured her."

"They'll want to finish the job," Catriona said under her breath. "I can bring them here. And I can be ready when they show up."

"Okay," Maureen said skeptically, "but can you be sure~"

Catriona stood up from the booth, taking the notebook with her.

"I'll be ready," she said again.

Catriona sat in the armchair in her apartment and stared at the notebook on her thigh. She'd spent countless hours in this chair. Recuperating. Healing. Feeling her body knit back together through a haze of whatever painkillers Maureen had managed to bring her. She didn't know how many days passed. She didn't know if the dark parts were night or unconsciousness.

She lifted her hand, spread the fingers out, and tried to see if any of them looked crooked or misshapen. They'd all been broken and reset. Some multiple times. Talking Man had once wondered aloud about cutting them off and reattaching them. Just to see if they could do it. "Let's see how much of you we can slice away before it becomes permanent," he'd whispered in her ear.

She didn't remember everything they'd done. She knew that was a blessing. She knew sometimes when she regained consciousness there were gaps she would never be able to recover. Sometimes her back would ache. Sometimes her throat burned, as if she'd been throwing up. The food they gave her was rancid, just enough to turn her stomach but not to kill her.

How much of her life had been lost because these assholes wanted a shortcut? Wanted her resources, but not her? She wondered how far the organization had tumbled in her absence. Without her in the field, how many missions had failed? How many bad things had happened because she wasn't around to do the worse thing?

She got up, her body remembering the days when rising from the chair had caused pain to burst from her knees, over her hips, flaming up her spine. She remembered when walking across the room had taken fifteen, twenty minutes, and ended with her drenched in sweat and gasping for air. Now she moved with purpose and retrieved the burner phone Maureen had gotten for her.

She went to the window and looked out at the street. She dialed a number she'd once known by heart and put it on speaker.

"Charles French and Associates, my name is Violet, how may I direct your call?"

"This is Catriona Hendrix. Tell the asshole in charge I'm finally ready to talk."

She disconnected the call and went to the table, where she removed the phone's SIM card and broke it. She then carefully and methodically took the entire phone apart, snapping pieces away from the whole and setting them aside before moving on to the next bit. When she was finished, she gathered all the smallest pieces and carried them into the bathroom to flush them down the toilet.

It wouldn't stop them from tracking the phone. She fully expected them to know where the call was coming from before 'Violet' even answered, but it felt enormously cathartic. The trace wouldn't be precise enough for them to find this address, but she was still going to have Maureen and Whitney relocate for a little while just in case. She didn't want either one of them getting caught in the crossfire when Silas showed up.

And she was confident he would show up. Maybe it wouldn't be Silas. Maybe it would be Robert or Benjamin or one of the others. Whoever showed up, though, she would know him. He would be Talking Man.

He'd left a job undone. And from what she'd learned about the man during their time together, she knew he would jump at the chance to finish it.

This time she would be ready.

The next day, Catriona paid for Ohanian's penthouse with a new credit card under her own name. As she expected, the management was more than willing to look the other way about the paperwork involved, but she made sure she was registered as the apartment owner. It made her wonder who had covered up Ohanian's death. Probably one of the other criminals in Seattle who was smart enough to know when a neighborhood was more trouble than it was worth. No one had rushed to take Ohanian's place, so she was confident saying the neighborhood was, for the time being, safe.

She paid extra to get access to the building security cameras, which she learned were located on the north, south, and east sides of the building, with a forth in the parking garage.

Once she had her security feed set up in the apartment, she packed a bag and went upstairs to wait. She bought a cell phone, also under her own name, and left it on the coffee table plugged into a charger.

Whitney and Maureen had relocated to a hotel, closing the Whipjack until further notice. Catriona paid for the hotel stay and made sure Whitney was compensated for the loss of income. She was, after all, entirely responsible for the danger that had run her out of her own home. Whitney was a good person. Compassionate. Even after Maureen confessed their crimes, Whitney was still willing to help them. Someone like that should be rewarded for seeing the good in people, even if it was just self-delusion.

Talking Man arrived three days after her call. She was impressed at his efficiency. He walked in like he'd been there a thousand times, completely casual in a suit and tie. He looked like a million other people she might have seen in downtown Seattle, but she'd seen that same slack expression on his face as he'd snapped her wrists. She knew not to let her guard down.

While he was in the elevator, Catriona went to the door and left it standing open. She moved to the sound system and cued up a song on repeat.

When Talking Man arrived at her threshold, David Bowie was singing "Queen Bitch" at half volume. Talking Man smirked and came into the apartment. He closed the door behind him, then held his blazer open and twisted one way, then the other, to show he didn't have any weapons tucked into his belt.

"I love Bowie," he said over the music, "but his early stuff was ah... hit and miss."

"I like 'Please Mr. Gravedigger', from his debut album," Catriona said. "Not a great song. But appropriate for the moment."

Talking Man smiled. "Because one of us is going to die here, is that right?"

"Silas, Franklin, Benjamin, Arthur, Robert."

He raised an eyebrow, and then snapped his fingers in understanding. "Ah. You figured out the names of the men in the room, but you don't know who is who. How is that possible?"

"Payroll, work assignments, people who worked for the organization with access to the location where I was held. I don't know all the parameters, but it took a while to find you all."

Talking Man nodded. "Well, it's impressive work, nonetheless. And accurate! There's no reason for me to not confirm you're right. Those were the men I assigned to take part in our little, ah, exit interview." He flashed her a smile and put a hand on his chest. "Arthur Ford, at your service."

Catriona took in a breath, held it, let it out slowly. Finally a name to go with the nightmares. But she kept her face neutral.

"So what's the plan here?" he asked. "I assume you're not stupid enough to think I came here alone. But I thought I would do you the courtesy of meeting you face-to-face, as requested, so we could put our unfinished business to rest."

"The unfinished business being you killing me."

He shrugged. "It's the standard retirement program with this profession. You knew that once, Miss Hendrix. Hell, you carried out a few of those retirements yourself, fully aware of who you were ending and why."

"Those people were eliminated because they got too old. They got sloppy. They grew a conscience. You decided I was done because I'm a woman. And that's the only reason you kept me alive and tortured me instead of just putting a bullet in my head. I'm still useful to you, and to the organization. You haven't been doing too well since you lost me as an operative, right? Failed missions. Operatives caught, imprisoned, executed. That's why you didn't kill me as soon as you knew where I was."

She moved closer to him.

"Last time we were face-to-face, you wanted my information. This time, you *need* it."

Arthur's smile remained fixed on his face. "You've proven yourself to be an extraordinarily talented operative, Miss Hendrix. You've managed to evade us for this long, and we both know I'm only standing here now because you wanted it to happen. The long and short of it is that we want you back. We know how much of an asset you are, we know the trials you've been through, and we're prepared to compensate you accordingly."

She held his stare. "I had proven myself while you were still checking your upper lip for new hairs, son. And the 'trials' I went through were all at your hand. On your orders. So the organization is willing to let me name my price to come back? Huh. That tells me a lot. That means there are probably people you have to answer to. Let's call them a council. And the council knew that I was the best agent they had on their payroll. And they were pissed when they found out you'd tried to eliminate me. Worse, I disappeared before you were able to get the information that made me so good. All those contacts, gone. And it was your fault."

Finally his smile began to waver.

"You aren't here to kill me, Arthur. You're here to beg me to come back to work for you. Are they listening? The people you brought with you?"

She saw his throat working as he swallowed hard, his eyes now cold. "Yes."

"Here's the deal." She raised her voice, just in case. "I'm dead. So is Maureen Rigby. Your man here killed us, put us both in the ground. So if your organization is suffering, it's his fault. I assume you're going to deal with his failure accordingly. I'll leave that up to you. And if you agree to leave me and my friend alone to rest in peace, I won't come after the other men I named. Considering everything else you've lost, the organization must be in shambles, and you can't afford to lose those men. But Arthur here? You'll be better off without him running things. Consider everything you've already lost under his leadership."

"What the hell do you think you're doing?" Arthur hissed.

"Killing you," Catriona said. "Not as hands-on as I'm used to, but it's just as effective in the end."

"They won't make a deal with you."

She raised an eyebrow. "Are you sure? How many men did they send with you? I'm sure they called it an assault force. A bunch of heavily armed men - probably only men, considering the way you run things - standing on guard, waiting for a signal. But then, fully aware of my location, they send you in. Alone. With a pathetic vest, like I wouldn't have gone for a headshot. They didn't even give you a weapon so you could prove you were just here to negotiate." She gestured toward the window. "Did they tell you they had a sniper locked on me? They probably did. I hate to tell you, buddy, but there's no sniper."

"You're just making all this up. You're guessing."

She laughed at that. "No. I'm remembering. Because I did this once in... ah, one of the Central American countries. It was a long time ago, and I didn't exactly go through the local airport. But I had a high value target and an agent I wanted to get rid of. He was a traitor. Long story. Doesn't matter. What's important is that I let him think he was running the show. I let him walk into the meeting with the big scary monster, and I listened as that monster killed him without interrupting his breakfast."

Arthur was breathing hard now, eyes darting around the room as if he expected operatives to pour out of every nook and cranny.

"There's nothing wrong with being a bad guy, Arthur. But it's a sin to be this fucking bad at your job."

He grimaced and reached up to work the top button of his shirt.

"I'm going to disappoint you boys now," Catriona said to their eavesdroppers. "I'm not going to kill him. I want him to run. I want him to have you breathing down his neck for the rest of his sure to be brief life. I want him to be scared."

Arthur had started backing toward the door. "They won't go for this."

Catriona tilted her head to the side and gave him a pitying smile. "They already have, Arthur. Because I was wrong about one thing."

She pointed and he looked down to see a red dot bouncing across the front of his shirt. He inhaled sharply and instinctively tried to swipe it away, then dived to one side so he was out of the line of fire.

"You can try to take me out hand-to-hand," she suggested, "but I think we both know how that would work out. And even if you did get lucky, you're just giving them more time to get into position. If you want to get past the lobby, I would suggest leaving as quickly as you can. And then... just run."

She could see his brain working, the gears spinning to calculate his chances. There was no possibility of him coming out on top.

Finally he took the option with the slightly higher chance of success and ran, flinging the apartment door open and disappearing down the hall.

Catriona calmly went to the door and closed it behind him. A minute later, the phone rang. She hadn't given anyone her number, so she knew who it had to be. She answered the call but didn't say anything.

"We expect you to hold up your end of the bargain, Miss Hendrix. The other men you named will not be harmed by you in any way. Do we have your word?"

She hated this deal. But she knew that going after them would only be slipping her own neck into the noose over and over again. The men had hurt her, yes, damaged her both physically and mentally in ways that might never fully heal. But they'd only been following orders, same as her. She could live with letting them go. Their careers had probably suffered greatly for their failure and for letting her get away. She didn't need to draw blood to get her vengeance on them so long as Ford, the man who had nuked her entire life, paid.

"Make him suffer, and we have an accord."

There was a brief silence. And then: "We have a deal. Our condolences, Miss Hendrix, on the loss of your handler. And the same to her on the loss of her operative."

Her lips quirked in an almost-smile. "I'll pass the sentiment along."

The phone clicked in her ear and Catriona disconnected on her end. She destroyed the phone as thoroughly as she had with the last one, flushing the components again.

When she was finished, she went to the window and searched the neighboring buildings for signs of the sniper. She knew they'd already be gone, but she had a fair guess which perch they'd been using. It was the same one she would have chosen. There might have been a moment when the laser sight had been fixed on her instead of Arthur, but that didn't bear thinking about. She'd convinced them of their plan, Arthur Ford would suffer for what he'd done, and the organization would forget she'd ever existed. She let the curtain fall back into place.

She was dead. She guessed it was time to figure out what to do with the rest of her life.

CHAPTER SIXTEEN

"CAN I ask how many people you've killed?"

Maureen shifted in the hotel bed, sliding her hand higher on Whitney's hip. She was silent for so long that Whitney held up one hand as if she could stop the question from existing.

"You can say no. I'm fine with not knowing. But if you're willing to say..."

"No, I'm willing. But I don't know an exact number, and I was wondering if that would be worse than any number I could say."

"Oh."

They were lying together on top of the blankets in the nicest bed Whitney had ever used, in the nicest hotel she'd ever stayed in. The curtains were open to take advantage of the gorgeous vista of Puget Sound, the sunlight reflecting off the water to make an especially golden spotlight for the curve of Maureen's hip. The glow also caught in her hair, highlighting and inflaming the redness to make it look unreal. It was also bright enough that Whitney could see all her freckles, and she idly traced her fingers along them as if she was tracing a hidden picture.

"Does it bother you?" Maureen finally asked.

"No," Whitney said. "I don't think I'm entirely okay with it. But I don't think it's enough to change how I feel about you. I saw you beat someone right in front of me, though that was hardly murder."

Maureen said, "Sometimes when I pulled the trigger, it was more ambiguous."

"Were there moments when, if you hadn't pulled the trigger, you would have been killed instead?"

"Yes. Every time, for the most part. But just because they wanted to kill me didn't make them evil."

Whitney rubbed her face. "Killing is wrong. I don't even like smashing bugs. Hell, I've perfected a way to escort flies out of my apartment so I don't have to swat them. It's a complex series of lamps and closing the curtains."

Maureen chuckled and cuddled closer to her. "You rescue flies. Of course you rescue flies. I love you so much."

Whitney took one of Maureen's hands and brought it to her mouth, kissing the fingertips and then letting the palm rest on her face like a mask.

"I don't care. I don't know if that makes me a bad person, and I don't know what it says about my morals, but the honest truth is that I just don't care if caring would mean I can't be with you. I can't change your past or who you are. But I can live with it."

Maureen sat up and brushed her nose against Whitney's cheek. "I love you, Whitney. And if I means I get to stay with you, I'll try to change. I'll get a different job. One with far less bloodshed."

"Then I'd suggest staying out of retail. You might not be able to restrain yourself."

Maureen laughed and kissed her.

Their morning had been spent briefly in the shower, mostly in the bed, and entirely in distracting themselves from thinking about what Catriona was doing across town. She'd told them to stay out of it. She had a plan, and she was confident it would work, but she wanted to be sure they were somewhere safe just in case something went askew. The sex was good and, for the most part, served its purpose to distract them, but in moments like this, worry kept slipping in.

"What about Catriona?" Whitney asked, looking to the window as Maureen rested her head on her chest. "If you do change, get a quiet, normal life, where does that leave her?"

"I don't know. But I don't think she'd go back to the organization. Once management tortures you and leaves you for dead, it's kind of hard to clock in on Monday. I'm sure she'll find something to do, but I doubt it will require a handler like me. I'll have time for a real life. I can take care of myself instead of worrying about someone else for a change."

Whitney hooked two fingers under Maureen's chin and raised her head so they were looking at each other.

"I'll worry about you, too. If you want."

Maureen smiled and nodded. "I want. I do."

They kissed again, and were in the midst of moving further when Maureen's phone rang. Whitney whined in frustration but patted Maureen on the hip, letting her know it was okay to answer. Maureen stretched to get the phone off the nightstand, dragging her hip along Whitney's thigh. Whitney took advantage of their new position to kiss and lick the outside curve of Maureen's breast. Maureen giggled and hissed for her to stop as she answered the call and put it on speaker.

"Catriona?"

"It's over."

Whitney stopped and twisted her neck to look at the phone. Maureen repositioned herself and rolled to the side of the bed, standing up and moving to stand in front of the window.

"Someone showed up?"

"Yeah. He's been taken care of. I'm going to keep an eye on things. Make sure everyone sticks to the deal we've made. You and Miss Mercer are safe where you are. I just wanted to let you know things are dealt with. I'm okay."

Whitney sat up in bed, watching Maureen's back. She was standing naked in front of the window, and she looked literally angelic. She had her head bowed, the hand that wasn't holding the phone curled in a fist in the small of her back.

"I appreciate that, Catriona," she said finally.

"For now, sit tight. I'll be in touch. I know Whitney is probably eager to get home."

Maureen looked over her shoulder and saw how Whitney was eyeing her. She smirked. "Don't rush on her account."

"We'll talk soon."

The call ended on that. Maureen disconnected and turned to face Whitney, staring down at the screen.

"She never calls just to let me know she's okay. She once had to destroy her computer on a mission in Dublin, and I didn't know she was alive until she walked into the building two weeks later like nothing had happened."

"The woman *did* basically die and come back to life," Whitney reminded her. "Maybe you're not the only one who is looking forward to a little change."

"Maybe..."

"Well, for now she said to sit tight." Whitney swept her hand across the mattress next to her. "No reason to worry now that you know she's okay."

Maureen grinned, returned the phone to the night stand before joining Whitney in bed.

Violet hesitated on the threshold of the Whipjack, her bag hanging off one shoulder and her hand on the door to keep it open. Whitney finally noticed her and raised an eyebrow.

"What, were you raised in a barn?"

"What?"

"Holding the door open like that... you'll let the cows out." Violet looked confused, so Whitney waved her off. "Folksy humor. You can come in. You *do* still work here."

Violet came in and let the door fall shut behind her. "Do I? Because you gave me a whole lot of money to just sit at home and study. We can keep doing that if it's easier for you. It's worked out pretty well for me."

Whitney smiled. "Sorry. You're going to have to start earning your paycheck again. Welcome back, and happy to have you."

Violet put her bag on the bar and looked at Maureen's empty booth. "So everything is... settled? All the weird stuff you had going on?"

"Weird stuff?" Whitney said. "I'm not sure what you're talking about."

"Hah," Violet said. "I watched the news. I saw things online. Dead bodies in the street. Ohanian suddenly vanished. You expect me to believe your new girlfriend and the weird tenant upstairs didn't have anything to do with that?"

Whitney rested her hands on the bar and tilted her head to the side. "I can say no, and we can leave it at that. Or I can explain everything, at which point you'd know everything. I'll leave it up to you. Which would you prefer?"

Violet sighed and shrugged. "Reporting for duty, boss."

"Great to hear it," Whitney said. "Oh, and since Bridgeman isn't going to be an issue anymore, I decided to spread that monthly expense across the rest of the budget. Five hundred of it is going to a raise for you."

"Really?" Violet said. "That's so generous. Are you sure?"

Whitney shrugged. "Like I said when I gave you the first bonus. You're worth it, and you've always been willing to wait a few days for your paycheck."

"Thank you, boss."

"You're welcome, Violet."

Violet went behind the bar and retrieved her apron, wrapping it around her waist. "So, uh, if we're really back to normal, we get to spend all day gossiping about your new girl? I don't think I even know her name."

Whitney said, "Maureen. Reena, sometimes, although I don't really call her that very much. I like her full name." She cleared her throat. "And no. We're not talking about her."

"Uh-huh," Violet said. "We'll see..."

They went about the work of setting up for the day, chatting about nothing in particular, mostly Violet catching Whitney up on what she'd been up to with school and romantic interests. After the insanity of the past few months, she reveled in the normalcy of the stories.

When the door opened with a quiet chime of bells, Whitney said, "Sorry, we're not open yet," before she realized the man who'd come inside was holding up his hands in surrender. After noticing that, she realized she recognized him. He was one of the goons who had sometimes come in with Bridgeman to collect the monthly payment.

"I don't want to cause any trouble."

"Then find another place to drink," Whitney said.

He held his hands out as if she hadn't seen them. "My name is Colin—"

"I don't care. Get out."

"Can I just... Will you hear me out? Please?"

Whitney tightened her jaw and looked at Violet. "Go in the back."

"Are you sure?"

"Yeah. I can handle myself."

Violet reluctantly went to the kitchen.

Colin said, "You won't have to handle anything. I swear. I just..." He swallowed and looked around. "I-is she here? She's not here, right?"

"Who?"

"Come on. You know who. Bridgeman may've been an idiot, but not all of us were. The lady who attacked us, you hired her. Is she here?"

Whitney rested her hands on the bar. "If you're so worried, the faster you say what you came here to say, the sooner you can get the hell out."

Colin inhaled and let it out slowly. "You think you did something good, don't you. Got rid of the big scary monster who was terrorizing the neighborhood. But that's not how it was. We really did offer protection."

She laughed. "I've gotten robbed six times since Bridgeman started screwing with us. You guys didn't do jack to stop that."

"Some junkies waved around a gun to get a fix, whatever, who cares. We're not going to patrol like a damn neighborhood watch. You might not have seen the benefits, but that doesn't mean we weren't making a difference."

"Who benefited from your so-called vigilance?"

"You know that massage parlor down the block? The guy who runs it is a piece of shit. But he's a coward, and he was terrified of Ohanian. So he was terrified of Bridgeman, and us, and what we would do if one of his girls said he was... you know... taking liberties. If they went to the cops with that, they'd say the ladies deserved it for being in that line of work. If they even bothered to show up at all. But Ohanian would have us break the guy's kneecap for the first offense, and he'd get more creative after that. The guy in charge is still there. And he knows Ohanian is gone, and he knows the cops still don't give a shit about this neighborhood."

Whitney felt a sense of dread that he might have been telling the truth, but she hoped it didn't show on her face.

"Even assuming you're telling the truth–"

"Hey, you got no reason to believe me. I know that. I'm just telling you before I hit the road and get out of town. We were criminals, there's no questioning that. You were probably right coming after us the way you did. At least on paper. But sometimes, in some places, a scarier bad guy is the best you can hope for to protect you from the other bad guys out there."

With that, he checked over his shoulder and fled from the bar.

Violet came out of the kitchen. "Do you think he's telling the truth?"

"That there are still assholes out there who were scared of the bogeyman, and getting rid of him is just going to encourage them?"

She crossed her arms and sighed wearily. "I've lived in this neighborhood all my life, and... it does make a lot of sense."

"Even so," Violet said, coming out behind the bar. "It doesn't make it your responsibility to do something about it. I mean, those guys caused a lot more trouble than they solved. They terrorized people. Destroyed businesses. Burned places down. You absolutely did the right thing, Whitney, no matter what happens afterward."

Whitney patted Violet's arm. "Thank you for saying that. Doesn't make it feel any better to sit around and ignore what's happening, though."

She asked Violet to finish prepping and went upstairs. She knocked on the door to Catriona's apartment and took a step back, staring at her shoes, wondering what she was going to say. When the door opened, she raised her eyes to meet Catriona's.

"There's something you need to check out."

Catriona narrowed her eyes.

Chapter Seventeen

THE RECEPTIONIST told her to go down the hall and wait in Room 3. Catriona closed the door behind her, sat down on the bed, and examined the cramped space. It reeked of oils and incense, although after a minute or two she decided the smell really wasn't that bad. Soft New Age music was piping through speakers in the ceiling. She thought about the cops who had been more than eager to help her out when Ohanian's hired guns showed up. She found it odd that the manager wouldn't be scared one of the girls would spill the beans to them. But then again, trusting a corrupt cop to fall on the right side of sexual abuse was never a winning bet. Hell, they might have helped out just so they could also get a free pass with the girls.

The door opened and a masseuse came in. She looked terribly young, with a stud on one side of her nose and far too much makeup. She smiled and moved toward the side table.

"You can go ahead and undress," the girl said as she began preparing her supplies.

"I'm not here for a massage."

"That's fine," the girl said without turning around. "But we still have to go through the process. You know, for the optics of the whole thing."

Catriona said, "I'm not here for that, either."

The girl finally looked at her. "What? Are you a cop? You should've told Hannah up front. We give discounts for cops."

Catriona sighed. "I'm nobody. I'm just a dead woman."

The masseuse turned and looked at her, curiosity piqued.

"What's your name?"

The girl hesitated. "Scarlet."

"Fine." Catriona rolled her eyes. "Your manager's name is Bud Kay."

Scarlet's nostrils flared, her eyebrows twitched up, and her lips pressed together. It was the quickest of reactions, but one it would've been impossible for Catriona to misread. Scarlet reacted to the name as if Catriona had pulled out a gun.

"Okay. That's one question answered..."

"You didn't ask a question," Scarlet said.

"Second question," Catriona continued, "is he here right now?"

Scarlet nodded once before she considered why she might be asking. "Don't complain. Please." She moved forward and reached for Catriona's belt. "I like girls. I prefer them." She dropped her voice to a husky whisper. "I got so excited when Hannah told me you were older. I can call you mommy if~"

"Don't," Catriona said. "I'm not going to complain. But I want you to tell me the truth. I'll only be mad at you if you lie. Understood?"

Scarlet nodded and took a step back.

"How often does Bud touch you and the other girls?"

Scarlet's face darkened. "I don't want to talk about that."

Catriona said, "Has it gotten worse since Ohanian went away?"

"Ohanian went away?" Scarlet said. "Shit. That explains..." She swept a hand over her face, into her hair. "I thought Bud had just finally grown a spine or something."

"So that's a yes."

Scarlet looked at Catriona again. This time there was no veil between them, no play-acting, and she could see real hardness behind the wide blue eyes. Catriona felt like this was the first time she was actually seeing "Scarlet," or whatever her real name might be.

"Who are you?"

Catriona said, "I'm the one who messed up and made things worse for you. I'm here to make them better."

Scarlett tucked her bottom lip into her mouth and looked at the door.

"How many girls are here right now?"

"Four, including Hannah."

Catriona said, "Clients?"

Scarlet shook her head. "I don't know."

"Okay. Where's Bud's office?"

"Down this hall at the very end, to the left. He usually leaves the door open."

Catriona nodded. "Okay. It's probably best for you to stay in this room."

"What are you going to do?"

"Sometimes I like to figure that out in the moment."

She slipped out into the hall again, checked to make sure no one was coming from the front of the building, and headed for the back.

The office door was open as promised. Bud Kay was sitting at a desk just inside the door. Behind him she saw a beaten-down sofa under a Wall of Fame of framed photos that showed Bud with his arm around various disgraced celebrities. He was currently hunched over, looking at a phone which thankfully had the screen angled so she couldn't see it. His back was hunched, he had a combover and a poorly tended beard, and his shirt looked like it had gone a week or two without going through the laundry.

"There's a problem with one of your girls," she said.

His head snapped up and he started to rise, responding to the words before he realized they were spoken by a stranger.

Catriona stepped into the office and shoved him, hard, while he was still halfway up and off-balance. He tumbled to the floor like a deck of cards. Catriona crowded into the room and kicked the door shut behind her. She dropped a knee on his chest, pinning him to the floor, and wrapped her hands around his wrists when he tried to reach up to grab her. They struggled for a few minutes, but Catriona clearly had superior strength and the upper hand. Bud eventually gave up and collapsed back onto the floor, panting heavily.

When he stopped fighting, Catriona rested all her weight on his chest and pulled his arms hard with both hands. Bud howled as his shoulders were dislocated. She released his arms, but they remained raised, the elbows bent and fingers curling in agony.

"Wh-who the h-h-h-hell are you?" he whimpered.

Catriona punched him in the face. She hit him again, then a third time. Once she decided his bell had been truly rung, she grabbed his collar and lifted his shoulders up off the floor.

"You need a bogeyman?" she hissed. "Fine. I'm your new bogeyman. If I hear a whisper of your employees being mistreated, even by a customer, I'll come back and I'll finish the job. You thought Ohanian was scary? I killed him because I was bored. Imagine what I'd do to someone who made me angry. Nod to let me know you understand."

His eyes were closed, and blood had spilled from his nose across his lips. He nodded, a feeble dip of his chin followed by a groan.

Catriona dropped him and stood up. "Don't disappoint me, Bud."

She turned and left the office. The door to Scarlet's room was open and she was peeking out. She started to retreat, but Catriona held up a hand to motion her forward into the hall. Scarlet hesitated but then came to her.

"Is anyone here against their will?"

Scarlet furrowed her brow. "What? Like prisoners?"

Catriona gestured at the other doors. "I'm just making sure everyone who works here is doing it by choice."

"Oh. Oh!" She tensed and looked around. "I mean. I-I think so? I know the money is great and the bad parts aren't really bad enough to make me leave. Hell, it beats working at Starbucks or whatever. A-and I don't think I've heard anything about anyone else. I can ask, though."

"Let me know. I'll give my number to the girl at the counter. Hannah?"

"Mm-hmm." Catriona stepped around her. "Hey, wait. Are you a cop?"

"No," Catriona said without stopping or turning around.

Scarlet said, "Then what are you?"

"Like I said earlier. I'm just a dead woman trying to fill her days. Be safe, Scarlet."

The move wasn't as dramatic as Whitney might have hoped. It felt like she and Maureen had been living together for ages, but she knew it had really only been a couple of weeks. And Maureen, like Catriona, traveled light. She only had a handful of outfits, all of which fit in her duffel bag. The majority of things she had to collect were laptops, phones, and chargers. Whitney was surprised to see how many of the devices had appeared in her apartment during Maureen's relatively short residence.

"Are you sure you want to leave?" Whitney asked as Maureen put the last phone in her pocket. "I don't mind having you here."

Maureen smiled and went to her. "I know. But I think if we're going to make an honest attempt at a relationship, we need to take a step back. Give each other a little space. Do the dating thing properly." She put her arms on Whitney's shoulders and kissed her nose. "I've never really dated anyone. I'm really looking forward to it."

"I'm looking forward to dating you, too," Whitney said.

"Besides. I'm not going very far." She went back to the couch to get her bag. "I'll just be down the hall in Catriona's place. I have an in with the landlady."

Whitney said, "Just be careful. I hear she can be really strict about rent."

Maureen turned, her expression worried. "Oh no. I might be late with this month's rent. I wonder if there's anything I can do to earn a little mercy from her."

"A little mercy?" Whitney asked, slipping her hands under Maureen's sweater. "Mercy?!"

She started tickling, and Maureen laughed and tried to slip away. Whitney was relentless, and ended up wrestling her down onto the couch. Eventually Maureen took off the sweater in an attempt to tangle Whitney's hands, and Whitney's shirt and tank top were also discarded in the scuffle. By the time it ended, Maureen's bag was on the floor under a pile of their clothes. Whitney was lying on top of Maureen, trying to catch her breath as she drew shapes the soft skin under her ribs.

"There's a lot to be said for having your own space. Somewhere you can go to just get away, get some solitude."

"Mm-hmm." Maureen played with Whitney's hair.

"And there's a lot to be said for sneaking into my apartment in the middle of the night and finding fun ways to wake me up."

Maureen laughed. "Definitely potential."

Whitney sat up and looked at her. "I'll miss you, though. Even though you'll be right next door. I've gotten used to looking over and seeing you in that booth."

"Maybe I can still work there some days. There's no reason I have to be tied to the office, especially since Catriona probably won't be there most of the time."

"I look forward to it." She dragged her fingertips up to the curve of Maureen's breast, circling the nipple with her thumb. "Do you think it'll work? Catriona's plan?"

Maureen let out a shaky sigh and licked her lips. "I don't know. I think it has potential. Someone had to come in and fill the vacuum Ohanian left. Better her than someone worse."

Whitney bent down and touched her lips to Maureen's breast. "I don't think you can call yourselves bad guys anymore."

"We're still not the good guys," Maureen said, now breathing hard and stroking Whitney's hair. "We're hurting people. It's not... ah... it's not okay just because they're bad people."

"Sure it is," Whitney said. "They win because they ignore the rules. The only way they can be beaten, really beaten, is to stop playing the game and make your own rules."

"It's a fine line."

Whitney shook her head. "There's no line. Not really, not in real life. You make your choices based on the situation, and you stick by them until you have a reason to change your mind. You make your path one day and one decision at a time."

"Mm-hmm." Maureen's eyes were closed.

Whitney smiled and moved down Maureen's body. "For instance, I consider myself a good person. But I'm about to do some very bad things to you..."

Maureen inhaled sharply and arched her back as Whitney started to demonstrate.

"I guess good and bad is just... in the, um... eye of the beholder..."

Whitney laughed.

Catriona looked out the window of what had once been Krikor Ohanian's office. She'd cleaned it out of everything he'd left behind, tossing most of it in the dumpster in the alley, but she had yet to replace anything but the basics. She had an old desk Maureen had found at a pawn shop, and chairs that were acquired at a yard sale the previous weekend.

There was no reason for her to have an address, to have a place where she went every day and sat behind a desk, but Maureen convinced her it was important to send a message to everyone in South Park. Ohanian was gone, but the neighborhood was still protected. There was someone looking out for them.

She didn't feel particularly safe staying in one place. Maureen was keeping an eye on the organization, along with the remaining four men who'd tortured her. She would be alerted if any of them came within a hundred miles of Seattle. The safety net did nothing to alleviate her anxiety. She looked down at her hands. Her fingers were healed. They were mostly straight, unbruised, and without pain even after the beating she'd given to Bud Kay.

She flexed and then made fists. She wasn't at full strength. She needed to figure out an exercise regimen. Maybe once she felt more like herself, once she felt strong enough to defend herself, she would relax. But until then...

There was a soft knock on the door. The plan had been for Maureen to act as her receptionist, but she was currently at home with Whitney. Catriona pulled the chair out from behind the desk and sat down. She smoothed her hands over the wood, scanned the now-empty bookshelves, then looked at the door.

"Come in."

After a brief hesitation, the door cracked open and a woman stuck her head inside. She looked around as if she expected to see a line of people along the back wall of the office. When she confirmed they were alone, she came inside and closed the door quietly behind her.

"Is your name Catriona Hendrix?"

Catriona nodded.

"I'm friends with Scarlet Derriford. You... she said you met her where she works? And you said you could help people who were, um, being treated badly...?"

"That's right. Do you work with her?"

The woman shook her head and came closer. "No. But I... I'm..."

"You're in trouble," Catriona said.

"Yeah," the woman said, so softly it was almost a whisper. Catriona gestured at one of the chairs in front of her.

"Have a seat," she said. "Let's see how I can help you."

ABOUT THE AUTHOR

Geonn Cannon is the author of over fifty novels, including the Riley Parra series which was adapted into an Emmy-nominated webseries by Tello Films. He's also written two tie-in novels for the television series Stargate SG-1. He was the first male author to win a Golden Crown Literary Society Award for his novel Gemini, and he won a second for Dogs of War. Information about his other works and an archive of free stories can be found online at geonncannon.com.